About the Author

David Callaway is a journalist and media executive with
more than forty years of news experience in the U.S. and
around the world. He's a former editor of *USA Today* and
of *MarketWatch* and a former chief executive officer of
TheStreet, Inc. He's also a former president of the World
Editors Forum, a Paris-based media freedom organization.
He's currently the founder and editor of *Callaway Climate
Insights*, a newsletter about climate entrepreneurs and
investors. This is his first novel. He lives in Marin County,
California, with his wife, Nanci.

Un-regulated Militia by David Callaway

David Callaway

Un-regulated Militia

Vanguard Press

VANGUARD PAPERBACK

© Copyright 2025
David Callaway

The right of David Callaway to be identified as author of
this work has been asserted by him in accordance with the
Copyright, Designs and Patents Act 1988.

A CIP catalogue record for this title is available from the British Library.

ISBN 978-1-83794-588-7

This is a work of fiction. Names, characters, businesses, places, events and
incidents are either the products of the author's imagination or used in a
fictitious manner. Any resemblance to actual persons, living or dead, or actual
events is purely coincidental.

Vanguard Press is an imprint of
Pegasus Elliot Mackenzie Publishers Ltd.
www.pegasuspublishers.com

First Published in 2025

Vanguard Press
Sheraton House Castle Park
Cambridge England

Printed & Bound in Great Britain

Dedication

To my wife, Nanci, and daughter, Alexandra, who make every new day a thrilling adventure.

Acknowledgments

To all the journalists I've worked with who covered and witnessed America's endless parade of active shootings over the decades and who reported on the powers that be in Washington and on Wall Street, who prevented us from finding a solution to a deadly problem of our own making. And to my father, James T. Callaway, who hooked me on writing and on the newspaperman's way of life.

Chicago never looked so good. Humming over Lake Michigan at seventy miles an hour, Fire Bird One sped toward the setting sun and Grant Park, host to more than 400,000 revelers celebrating a newly elected President.

Fire Bird and twenty-four more armed drones zeroed in fifty feet over the dark blue November waves. Another squadron approached from the north, crossing the Chicago River over the Loop.

A festival atmosphere cloaked the impending chaos. Blues bands played and barbeques smoked with Chicago-style baby-back ribs and tri-tip. Students danced and waved American flags with the euphoric certainty of the young when convinced they've just changed the world. Older voters took photos and breathed the cold night air with the comforting satisfaction of a return to normal after four hard years in the opposition wilderness.

Brennan McCarthy took a deep tug from his vape and stared into the clear twilight sky. It was his first election as an eligible voter, and his side had won. It seemed like the whole country was celebrating that night, even though he knew half the populace was devastated. "Fuck them," he said to no one in particular. They had their chance.

On stage, a band played "Won't Get Fooled Again," by The Who as the crowd cheered and swayed. *So, this was what democracy felt like*, McCarthy thought. Shortly, a new president would address the crowd, and then he and his friends would spend the rest of the night partying to celebrate their good fortune.

McCarthy began to turn and reach for another Old Style in the cooler when he saw the lights.

The drone forces connected just off the windy beach below the river, turned south as one, and, descending to twenty-five feet, strafed the crowd over more than half a mile, raining bullets for more than twelve straight seconds before turning skyward.

Music and excited political chatter quickly turned to screams and stampeding panic as the crowd broke loose in all directions. Bodies were everywhere on the frozen ground, bleeding into Olympic Goose overcoats as loved ones searched for each other and police tried to make sense of what had just happened.

"It was as if gunfire came from the ground," Office Tim McNealy radioed back to the 4th District Precinct. "Hundreds are down. Hurry."

McCarthy's twenty-year-old body lay trampled in the mud, his vape still clutched in his left hand, six bullets in his torso, and a stunned look in his eyes, which had never before seen danger. His friends had fled or were lying beside him bleeding.

It was only as the crowd scattered and police surveyed the line of dead and wounded, that they realized the shots had come from the sky. Some people said they saw what looked like a flock of birds, but they moved so fast they couldn't be sure. Videos began to emerge of tracer lights from the gunfire. Network footage fueled the early reporting. Grant Park had been attacked!

Chicago was no stranger to random violence. It had been the murder capital of the U.S. for more than a decade now, with more than two thousand gun-related deaths each year, surpassing New York of the late 1970s. Political history, from the 1968 riots at the Democratic Convention under the heavy fist of Mayor Richard Daly's machine to the rise of Jesse Jackson and Barack Obama, had a special place in Chicago.

In recent years, though, many had hoped that would change. The election night speech of President Obama in 2008 had energized the nation, and now President-Elect Virginia 'Ginny' Robinson, the first black woman to win a Presidential election, was set to stake her claim to that legacy with a similar grand event.

Even though she was from California, Robinson had chosen Grant Park and Chicago, the same place Obama had given his speech, to show respect to her pioneering predecessor. Her helicopter was only twenty minutes away. As the first reports came in, the copter was diverted to a secure section of O'Hare Airport and hustled into a protected hangar.

The President-Elect watched videos of the scene on a desk screen in her cramped office onboard. All her political life—all her life—she had fought against the senseless use of guns by American citizens on each other. Her campaign, the first to really put gun violence front and center, had been the most divisive and downright threatening of the series of polarized Presidential campaigns going back to the Reagan years.

Now, on the eve of her triumph, as she prepared to address the American people for the first time as President-Elect, Robinson was prepared to finally put an end to the random slaughter that had earned her country the scorn of the entire world.

Instead, a nation well opiated from a steady stream of gun violence and home-grown horror faced a new crisis: Gun terror from the sky.

Chapter 1

"A well-regulated militia, being necessary to the security of a free state, the right of the people to keep and bear Arms, shall not be infringed." – Second Amendment of the U.S. Constitution

Pearson Willis made the sign of the cross and pushed himself up on creaky knees. For more than thirty years, he'd been praying at the hundred-year-old Saint Clement Church in Lincoln Park. This Thursday was no different. He never failed to marvel at the Byzantine architecture of the altar and walls where he worshiped. He was lost in their beauty and filled with peace as his shoes echoed down the aisle toward the door. Outside, the sun was shining, and he lowered his gaze to adjust his eyes as he descended the church steps.

The bullet hit him square in the temple.

Willis was dead before he thudded to the ground, a puddle of blood rippling from his head as shocked onlookers rushed to help.

"What happened," shouted one teenage girl.

"Don't know," an older man responded as he looked for a pulse. "He just collapsed. I heard a shot, but it was way over there," he said, motioning toward Lincoln Ave. "Call 911!"

Minutes later, as Chicago police stretched the yellow tape around the crime scene, Willis' sister came running into the crowd and draped herself over him. "This ain't right. This ain't right," she screamed. "What was he doing? An old man coming out of the church. What was he doing?"

Willis was the 1,947th shooting victim in Chicagoland this year, as the city careened toward another national record in killings. Most were with unregistered guns, as gangs vied for territory in the city's west and south sides. Occasionally, the violence bled into the more upscale Gold Coast, and Lincoln Park. Long known for its crooked police force, the city had begun in the last decade to enter a Wild West era of shootings and revenge killings, not unlike The Troubles of Northern Ireland in the 1970s. The police would or could do little except stretch the tape and tally the numbers.

Lieutenant Dale Ramsey looked down as the stretcher carried Willis' lifeless body to a waiting ambulance. "This one's not even worth investigating," he said quietly to one of the paramedics.

In his twenty-two-year career in the CPD, Ramsey had never seen so much random violence. The 1980s gangs of Cabrini Green had evolved into more sophisticated crime operations, while those left behind fended for themselves. The war was fueled by a never-ending supply of guns, many legal, as citizens seeking to protect themselves and their families fought a running battle with, well, everyone else.

Ramsey himself owned more than a dozen guns, of all makes, in his Southside home. More than once, he crouched at his upstairs window with his rifle poking out a crack, looking for the source of loudening gunfire. Especially during the time of the coronavirus a few years back. He was determined to protect his home, and he took his job seriously as part of that.

The city was still in shock over the mass killing two days earlier of 372 people at the Robinson celebration in the Lower Loop. The FBI and Secret Service had immediately taken over the investigation, trying to determine if it was foreign terrorists or a homegrown operation, which would have been the largest since the Oklahoma bombing of 1995. But who?

Ramsey was sure it was a well-organized, paramilitary operation, likely from out of state, intending to send Robinson an early message that her gun control promises to the electorate were dead on arrival. It had come to this.

As he drove home that night, glancing in the mirror as he arrived on West Jarvis Ave., Ramsey pondered how America had arrived at this spot in history, where citizens were killing each other in a sort of undeclared civil war over their right to kill.

A student of military history, he could think of no similar time in the past where citizens of a country literally tore themselves apart. He was glad he had his guns. Just in case they came for him.

He would need them in the coming days.

***

In the WBBM newsroom in the Loop, Lindsey Hoken's eyes glazed over when a city editor mentioned the Willis murder. Another stranger shot by a stranger was not the story she wanted today. President-Elect Robinson, diverted immediately on reports of the Grant Park shooting two days before, had returned to Chicago to lend support to the recovery and stand with the families of the dead. Hoken had worked hard to convince her campaign staff to give WBBM a few minutes, and she was hoping to hear back in an hour. Everybody was on the Grant Park story but her.

Hoken particularly wanted to grill Robinson on her controversial position advocating for the seizure of guns. For years, Democratic candidates had been careful to focus on gun control. The sales process of arming America. Not the removal of some three hundred million existing guns. It was the one thing the gun lobby feared most, and the reason it was rabid in never giving an inch.

"Remember Berlin" was one rallying cry, a reference to Hitler's order requiring all public citizens to turn in their firearms. Once he had achieved this, the public was little match for his Brownshirts, and Germany was on a path to war and ruin. There would be no second time. Led by the powerful National Rifle Association, pro-gun Americans had begun resisting by organizing privately and protesting publicly. Charlottesville, Atlanta, Boise, Colorado Springs—all sites of protests gone horribly wrong.

Robinson advocated taking guns away, through public buybacks, as well as tax and regulatory pressure on gun sellers, gun ranges, and even hunting. Hoken didn't see how she would get any of those proposals through a reluctant Congress.

"No way any of her ideas get passed now," Hoken said to her desk mate. "I want to be the first to make her admit it."

Hoken stood out in the WBBM newsroom in that she understood and supported the logic of the Second Amendment. Raised in the Upper Peninsula of Michigan, Hoken was a 'Yooper' of French-Canadian descent, who learned to shoot early on in her family's logging community.

She was a voracious reader whose favorite book was *'Last of the Mohicans,'* set in upstate New York during the French and Indian War. She particularly loved Hawkeye, the scouting hero of the book who was nicknamed La Longue Carabine, or The Long Rifle, by the French-speaking Huron Indian tribe. As a teenager, she would spend hours running through the woods with her own Remington Model 783 Bolt-Action rifle, shooting at rabbits and squirrels as if they were Hurons.

Hoken's curiosity and reading and writing prowess eventually pulled her out of the woods and into Northwestern University's Medill School of Journalism in Evanston, Ill., then to a small suburban newspaper before landing the plum job at Chicago's leading all-news station.

She had started, as most journalists do, as a general assignment reporter at night, which meant working with the cops. But lately, she had moved to the politics desk, covering Mayor O'Neill and the Chicago City Council. The Robinson interview was her big shot. She had been given the President-elect's private phone number in her phone and was just waiting for the signal to call. Instead, she was on her way to Lincoln Park to cover another stupid shooting.

"What's the point?" she wondered to her desk mate as she gathered her purse and coat. "If the police aren't going to do anything they'll just be another one tomorrow."

As she left the building, she checked her bag to make sure her Ruger LC9 pistol was there. She patted it like a small dog.

***

Armand Barry Johnson watched CNN with a small smile on his face. Sitting in his office in Denver, the billionaire investment executive and political power player enjoyed the confused reporting and uninformed speculation. That's when money got made.

Chicago police and the Feds were focused on homegrown terrorism, which meant they would round up the usual suspects: local drone owners, various small airport operators, gun rights advocates in Illinois and nearby states, and local mob leaders.

From his perch on the 54th floor of the Republic Tower, he thought he could just make out the red-tile roof of his mansion in the foothills thirty miles away in Evergreen. Like most cities after the Chicago massacre,

Denver was on police lockdown, with all private aircraft grounded until further notice. Johnson didn't care. He wasn't going anywhere today.

"Mr. Johnson, Don Bingham here for your two-thirty," his secretary, Natalie, sang into his phone receiver.

"Send him in, Natalie."

"Army, you were right," Bingham said as he charged into the room. "Gun stocks were on fire this morning."

Johnson had built his investment fund company on stocks people loved to hate. Energy stocks, weapons makers, black ops consultants, booze. Especially energy stocks. As climate change roiled the headlines and traditional fossil fuel companies lost favor, Johnson invested heavily in them, guessing they would ultimately be asked to help solve the problem. The revival in energy stocks in the early 2020s was one of the great market surprises of its time, given the collapse of oil during the coronavirus scare, and Johnson and his clients were the ultimate beneficiaries.

Johnson himself didn't drink or smoke. Didn't like to travel, with the exception of his beloved marathons, which kept him fit. Didn't even shoot. He believed in the promise of America and that he was a shining example of that promise. Raised not far from his home in Evergreen, he was a high school football star who went on to an unspectacular college career at the University of Colorado, Boulder, which ended with a concussion in his junior year. With little specialized education to go on, he gravitated toward the markets in the late 1980s, which was where the excitement was, in his opinion.

He moved to New York City and landed a job at Merrill Lynch on the equities desk. He loved the rough-and-tumble of Wall Street, screwing clients and competitors on trades, then heading to Harry's after the close to swap loud lies with the Jersey and Long Island crowd over steak dinners. Lying came easy to Johnson. One day, the assistant on his desk, Donna Petrero from Staten Island, caught him lying about which deli he ordered his sandwich from.

"Why would you lie about something like that," she said.

"Practice," Johnson replied.

From Merrill, Johnson went on to Deutsche Bank, trading fixed income and currencies in the early 1990s, and then to the asset management side, where he became one of the top international fund managers in his category for five straight years. Having witnessed the rise of Michael Milken at Drexel a decade before, and envying his LA lifestyle, Johnson quit Wall Street and hung his shingle in Denver, close to the mountains he loved.

With his record, it was easy to quickly raise $2 billion in assets under management, and he went on from there. As a contrarian investor, sworn to go in the opposite direction of everyone else, Johnson scorned the rise of globalization. He was convinced the 'Davos Man' crowd and the elite financiers of New York, the UK, Hong Kong, and the like would ultimately steal all the money, leaving ordinary Americans—like his friends in Colorado—in the lurch.

Johnson's passion for making money at others' expense was topped only by his desire to knock the chips off the shoulders of the coastal elites and return America to its frontier roots. A nation where men were tough and armed. He was a heavy political donor and was wooed by up-and-coming conservative politicians across the country.

Johnson clicked off the video screen and leaned over his desk toward Bingham.

"What is our latest FANG position," he said, noting the acronym for the stocks of Facebook, Amazon, Netflix, and Google.

"About twenty percent," said Bingham. "We've been lightening it the last few weeks as you're asked."

"Tomorrow go short the whole basket," Johnson ordered.

"What do you mean? These stocks have been on a roll. You've been in them since almost the beginning," the younger executive said.

"Just do it. End of the day tomorrow," Johnson said, dismissing him with a wave of his hand.

As Bingham left, Johnson picked up the phone and dialed Reno.

Chapter 2

Hoken knocked on the door of Willis' dilapidated townhouse on W. Fletcher, on the outskirts of Wrigleyville. A Chicago Cubs World Series Champion banner from that magical season in 2016 strained in the wind above the doorway.

A young woman opened the door.

"We already talked to the police," she snarled.

"I'm with WBBM," Hoken said.

The young woman looked her up and down, not impressed with the snappily-dressed white woman in front of her.

"Get this," she turned and said over her right shoulder. "We got media now."

"Why don't you just leave us alone to grieve my father," she said, her eyes watery and red. "There's no story here. Just a good man killed for no reason. Happens every day around here."

Hoken was a young journalist, but she'd done enough door-stepping to know what to expect when you disturb a grieving family. It was always the same. The shock was so powerful they just wanted to be left alone. What they didn't understand was that the public's interest in their loved one—the story—was fleeting. Tomorrow there would be another killing. Another shooting. Another earthquake, plane crash, or terrorist attack. The time to tell the story of their loved one's life, of his or her passions and history, was now. And only now.

"Please, it's because he was a good man that I want to tell people his story. I won't disturb you for long."

The young woman wiped her eyes and grunted.

"Okay, just for a few minutes, you hear?" She pushed open the door and waved Hoken in.

The living room was dark and filled with the mementos of a life hard lived. Photos from Willis' time in the first Gulf War, on the tip of the spear. Awards from the plastics factory he worked at for thirty years. A few shots of family outings, usually to Wrigley Field to watch the Cubs when he could get away for a day game.

The woman, Keisha, sat in front of a dusty scrapbook, looking for photos for the funeral service. Around her sat her Uncle Darrell, Gillis' brother; his wife Sarah; their daughter Evelyn and Keisha's blond Labrador, Juno.

"He didn't deserve this. Didn't deserve it. Thirty years of service. Served his country. Union member. A dedicated member of the NRA. He was a man of the people. And they killed him," Keisha said.

"At least he got to see the Cubs win," said Darrell. "Most folks around here lived and died without even that."

"Was he a big fan?" asked Hoken.

"Yeah, loved to go to games. But mostly just listened on the radio or went down to Rose's to watch with his buddies. Never bothered anyone. Church, work, bar, family. He didn't deserve this."

"You said he belonged to the NRA," Hoken said. "Did he carry a gun?"

"Oh no. He's got one right there on his desk. An old Glock. But he never took it with him."

She stood and crossed the gray carpet to his desk. "Hey, it's not here. Darrell, you seen the Glock?"

"No, not in years actually."

"Maybe he has it up in his room or something," Sarah said. "Things get pretty loud around here at night."

"I'll go check," Keisha said.

As she walked up the creaking staircase, Hoken turned to Sarah and Darrell.

"I'm so sorry. It sounds like he was just in the wrong place at the wrong time," she said.

Before they could answer, Keisha screamed from upstairs. Darrell bounded ahead, followed by Hoken and Evelyn.

As they entered the room, Keisha was holding Gillis' Cubs hat, spattered in blood.

***

Lieutenant Ramsey was assisting FBI investigators in the lab when the call came. He was helping them identify the make and the history of the automatic weapons attached to the drone squadron. So far, the FBI was nowhere.

"What do you think, agent, uh…"

"Bledsoe, sir. Jim Bledsoe," said a twenty-something agent with short-cropped brown hair and thick glasses.

"They appear to be Ingram Mac10s, which if I remember my history right, were popular among far-right groups in the 1980s. They are essentially machine pistols, which make them lighter and easier to attach to the drones than semi-automatic rifles or proper machine guns."

"I don't think I've ever seen them," said Ramsey, peering over Bledsoe's shoulder at his forty-inch flat desk screen.

"They're quite rare these days. Most were sold before there were any real rules on ownership documents. That's going to make them harder to track."

"Organized drone squadrons attacking from the sky," Ramsey said to no one in particular. "Who would have thought?"

"It's actually not new, sir," Bledsoe said without turning his face from the screen. "Militaries have been using drones since at least the mid-1800s."

"Back then, they were balloons with explosives tied to them. The Austrians once used them to attack Venice. Didn't work very well as the wind kind of blew them in all directions. But a few of them hit. Caused quite a scene from what I read."

"Why weren't they developed in later wars?" Ramsey asked, his military curiosity piqued.

"They were, but more for surveillance reasons. The actual quadcopter format we see today was invented in the early 1900s, about the same time as the airplane. But the real development came with the advent of the model airplanes in the 50s," he said.

"Once folks could figure out how to control them from the ground and add radio controls, they progressed quickly from toys to military tools. We used them in Vietnam."

"You aren't even old enough to remember the first Gulf War, let alone Vietnam," Ramsey said.

"How do you know all this?"

"Video games," Bledsoe said proudly. "I was using drones to target evil space aliens and cyber dragons from the time I was five years old. Found my way into the military. Wanted to be a marine.

"Hoo-rah! and all that. But my eyes weren't good enough. So, I spent a few years in the Army under the DOD (Department of Defense) taking out terrorists in the Middle East from a base in upstate Connecticut. The drones we used were modern and cheap and could be directed from anywhere you had a signal.

"Ukraine used them to great effect in the war with Russia a decade ago, essentially making up for the lack of artillery they were able to get from Western allies.

***

For me, honestly, taking out the terrorists was easier than the cyber dragons. I needed a new challenge so I joined The Firm in new technologies."

While no foreign terrorist groups had claimed responsibility for the Chicago attack, no homegrown groups had stepped forward either. President Tom McHenry had vowed a moratorium on all gun sales a day after the attack, enraging gun supporters further and fueling a furious rush to load up in case the freeze was enacted.

Ramsey felt he was okay. He had his commissioned, 9mm Ruger on him, and his collection at home, some of which were loaded. When society in Chicago and other cities started to break down during the Great Cessation a few years back during the pandemic, some gangs started going house to house to loot and pillage. Those without protection suffered, and it led to further armament before the government was forced to have troops patrol the streets in some cities, which enraged gun owners even more.

The COVID-19 virus had briefly brought people together, but the economic effects of the shelter-at-home orders ripped them back apart, and violence was inevitable. By the time a vaccine came on the market early the following year, the U.S. had suffered more deaths than in World War I. Not all of them were from the virus. It was a time of lawlessness that evoked the old Wild West.

The Chicago Police had held the city together, but barely. In large parts thanks to men like Ramsey who had patrolled the streets and were not afraid to shoot first and ask questions later.

Ramsey's phone rang. He didn't recognize the mobile number but answered anyway, in case it had to do with the attack case.

"Lt. Ramsey, this is Lindsey Hoken; I'm a reporter with WBBM."

"How did you get this number?" he said, turning away from Bledsoe and the FBI technicians.

"I'm sitting with the Willis family here in Lincoln Park. You had given this number to Mr. Willis' daughter at the crime scene."

"I'm a little bit busy right now, miss. What did you say your name was?"

"Hoken. Lindsey Hoken. I think you should drop over when you get a chance. One of the family members just found something in the victim's room that makes this seem less of a random act."

I'll be the judge of that. Put the daughter on."

"Hello," said Keisha.

"Hi, this is Lt. Ramsey. How are you all doing?"

"Not so good, Lt. We just found a bloody hat in my dad's bedroom."

"He wasn't wearing a hat when he was killed, miss, uh…"

"Keisha. I know. But this was his favorite hat. He wore it almost everywhere, but not to church. I saw him wearing it just last week. Something happened to him before this shooting. We just don't know."

"I'll stop by on my way home tonight," Ramsey said. "Get that reporter out of there and we can take a look."

Ramsey hung up and cursed. The last thing he needed was petty domestic abuse or a neighborhood feud right now. He turned back to the FBI men.

"Anything else you boys need," Ramsey said.

"Yeah," said a red-faced investigator with a Boston accent. "Get your chief down on the line, now."

Chapter 3

It had been years since the college football game between USC and the University of California had been important, mostly since Cal had been so horrific. But a 6-1 season this year had Bears fans thinking of the Rose Bowl if they could get past the Trojans, also 6-1.

The excitement electrified the Cal campus in Berkeley, and the Indian summer weather that November Saturday hosted a packed tailgate scene on fraternity row. As drunken students mixed with alumni and their families to file into the ancient California Memorial Stadium, Graham Hughes and his girlfriend, Darla, climbed up the hill on the East Side to watch for free, as many students traditionally did.

Hughes was a junior at Cal, hailing from nearby Lake Tahoe and studying civil engineering. He'd been preparing for finals all week and was eager to take a break and catch the game, and to spend time with Darla before she headed home to Michigan for Thanksgiving.

The couple sat among friends and admired the sunshine on the Bay in the distance. A handful of girls on the next blanket, dressed in Cal sweatshirts and sweatpants, passed a vape and talked loudly about how hungover they were. Darla turned to Hughes.

"Some days just can't get more perfect," she said, leaning her head on his shoulder.

"It's pretty nice," he added. Now if these guys can put together a win, maybe we can spend New Year's in Pasadena."

Down on the field, Cal mascot Oski the Bear danced happily around to the music, teasing players and calling attention to himself as he prepared to confront the away-game version of USC's famous home mascot, Traveler the white horse.

Stephen Drake, a sophomore economics major, hated his weekend job as Oski. But it gave him free time during the week to attend his political clubs, and it was at least a way to get some exercise. Drake was not comfortable in the Berkeley universe. Raised in a conservative family from Kansas, he railed against the liberal extremists at the university and made a point of carrying his beretta pistol in his side pocket wherever he went, including in his Oski costume.

Drake fancied himself a hero and vowed he would be ready if ever called to arms against an invading force or local government. As with previous games, he'd had no problem strolling by security in his Oski suit without a metal check. But at the moment, concealed carry was the last thing on his mind. He was preparing to torment the Trojan horse.

Memorial Stadium was built into a hill. But it was also built right over the Hayward Fault, an offshoot of the more famous St. Andreas earthquake fault, which at 730-miles long was the largest in California. Thankfully, that piece of it had never ripped apart. The university had redone the field years ago to help prepare for that day, and cheekily included a line straight down the field to indicate where the fault lay. Legend had it the fault ran through the visitor's locker room.

But as the crowd stood for the Star-Spangled Banner, few imagined that tragedy would come from the sky instead of deep in the earth.

Hughes and Darla stood with the rest, mouthing the words. "And the rockets' red glare, the bombs bursting in air…"

Two miles away and closing fast over the East Bay were another forty drones, flying low beneath the radar of nearby Travis Air Force Base. Like a fly-by so admired by American sports fans, the drones revved down University Avenue toward the campus, rising just to the left of the stadium as they circled around the hill and dove toward their target.

Hughes and Darla had just turned toward the small cooler they shouldered up the hill with a thermos of Bloody Marys as applause met the last lines of the National Anthem when they heard the first shots. Spinning around, Hughes found himself at eye level with the drone squadron as the first bullets whizzed by him. He instinctively dove on Darla as the deadly turrets sped by and lifted his head to see the squad dip toward the field and the Western stands.

Hughes watched in slow-motion horror as the drones sliced across the field at the camera level, aiming directly at the opposing players as they stood absently gazing toward the American flag in the end zone. Unable to process what he saw; Hughes' first thought was whether the game might be delayed now.

Blood ripped through the stands as the band on the field and the USC team on the Western sideline scattered. The pock-pock-pock of bullets bouncing off the concrete mixed with screams of pain and fear as fans raced for the thin exits, which were still letting fans in.

Drake was playfully poking the USC horse when he heard the first shots. He turned his bulky costume toward the stands and stood gaping as the bullets sliced through the crowd, his Oski mask frozen in a goofy smile. He sank to his knees, unable to react, until he remembered his pistol.

Hughes's slow-motion experience exploded into real-time the second the bullets hit the visiting crowd, dissolving into amazement as he watched the bullets pierce through USC banners and hoodies, painted bodies, and cheerleader outfits. He was then startled at the unbelievable site of Oski the mascot down on one knee, firing a pistol into the air wildly.

Panic and fear met confusion and curiosity as a stampede of fans crushed their way toward the gates. Hughes watched as one young mother, a child in each hand and a carton of soda and hot dogs cradled in her left arm, was bowled over by the mob and disappeared between pounding feet.

What few sports doctors and med students there were at the game began to triage more than two hundred bodies sprawled in the stands, on the field, and on the hill. Others raised their phones to the sky to try to capture the fleeing drones.

In the instant it took the press and announcers in the press box, and security, to realize what had happened, the drone air force disappeared over the campus and back toward the Bay. Sailors near Marin County reported seeing them buzz over St. Quentin as they stayed low and followed the Bay toward Sacramento.

Drake emptied his gun and threw it down as two security guards raced toward him and tackled him, his Oski mask still on. As one of the guards pressed a knee into his back, he turned his head to the side and stared at the vacant gaze of a young USC cheerleader fifteen feet away, her torso bleeding in the chest and stomach. Her pom poms were still clutched in her hands.

Hughes glanced down at Darla, who was wincing in pain. She had a bullet wound in her shoulder and was grasping it while taking rapid, shallow breaths. He wrapped his bandana around her shoulder and told her to lay down while he desperately waved for help.

All around him on the hill, people had fled or were lying on Cal blankets, screaming in different levels of pain.

Hughes wondered if his other friends were okay. He needed to text his parents. He needed to get Darla medical help. He stared down at the carnage of what moments ago had been a Saturday afternoon, American tradition.

Then he got mad.

***

Ginny Robinson knew exactly where the Cal game attack took place.

As a young law student at the UC Berkeley School of Law, she remembered trudging from Boalt Hall after a Saturday morning study session to attend the games. Robinson was the first in her family to attend college, much less law school. After four years at UC Davis and two years as a paralegal in downtown San Francisco, she thrilled her family in Oakland by getting into Berkeley.

More than three decades later, after a successful law career that led her to Congress and now the White House, Robinson had been poised to finally make the changes to the country's staggering inequality problem that had dogged her family and those like it in Oakland and across the land for so long. Until now.

"Has the governor closed the airports yet, or scrambled the jets?" she asked the aide who had burst into her home office in Marin County. She knew it was too late to do anything about the drones, but the public needed to see action.

One horrific attack, on the night of her election, had been traumatic enough. Now the public would be scared everywhere. She remembered as a student the feeling after 9/11 that planes could come out of the sky and crash into her house, or her father's restaurant in Jack London Square. That desperate feeling in her chest, like she couldn't breathe right when she thought about how helpless she was when she walked into a store.

They say three makes a trend. But on terror attacks, one is enough, and two is war. Someone was sending her a message. But more than that. They were sending a message to the public. Arm yourselves. Your governments and your police cannot protect you.

"Gun sales are soaring this morning," the aide said. President McHenry's moratorium promise had lasted barely twenty-four hours before it collapsed in a hail of political outrage and black-market sales. How anyone with a pistol at the game could have stopped that drone army, Robinson could not imagine. But people would feel more comfortable with a sidearm now. Exactly what she didn't need.

Network footage and social media video now had a clear picture of how the drones had descended on the stadium and in which direction they left. They would have split up into scores of smaller groups, making tracking difficult. But the FBI could track the signals and provide a better idea of where some of them might be going. Hopefully in a few hours.

Robinson knew she had to go live that night and address the nation.

"The networks are jamming our phone lines. They all want a statement," the aide said. This was the mess she would inherit, after all, and she had no idea whether that was even the reason for the attacks. But the ball was still in President McHenry's court, as it was still two months before Inauguration Day.

She put her head in her sweaty hands and took a deep breath. "Wait for the President. It's his move," she ordered. No doubt McHenry would activate the National Guard in the Bay Area just as he had done in Chicago. A show of force against an enemy so far unwilling to show its hand.

That, of course, would jack up the tension, as the site of military on the streets would upset both liberals and conservatives alike. If this continued, her first hundred days would be consumed with stopping a civil war on the streets of every city in America. Assuming she got to those first hundred days. Some extremists were already calling for a delay in the Inauguration until the threat was better identified.

Robinson considered her family's security for a moment. Her husband Dwayne, also a lawyer, working downtown on the 32nd floor of the Bank of America building, an obvious target. Their one daughter, fifteen-year-old Joy, named after her mother, was at Marin Academy, only a ten-minute drive away. Added security was coming for each of them.

She switched to how she should alter her cabinet choices to account for this chaos. Homeland Security would now be top of mind. And her plans to clean up Wall Street and to rid the nation of guns would need to be put on hold – again.

Robinson looked out the window at the Marin Headlands, allowing herself a reflective moment to enjoy the wispy fingers of fog creeping down the hill toward Sausalito, a gentle stream of cloud announcing the end of the morning sun. She always marveled at how what the locals called 'Carl the Fog' ruled the micro-climates of the Bay, powering across the water some days and curling into the hills on others, oblivious to time and the trappings of wealth below.

The phone disturbed her.

"Yes," she said.

"Mrs. President-Elect, we have a message from Armand Johnson, we think you should look at."

Dear President-Elect Robinson,

No doubt you are as concerned about these recent attacks on our country as I am. While I am a major Republican Party donor, I believe at times like this we must put aside politics and focus on the safety of our country.

The mastermind behind these attacks has demonstrated he/she can strike anywhere. And to date, our technology has been unable to follow the drones. To me this indicates a military connection that is as threatening to our freedoms as it is to our lives. Only someone or group with access to the military's most advanced cloaking systems could command such a devastating force.

While I realize you are not yet President, I would hope that upon taking the oath, you'd be willing to work with me and an elite group of my friends from the financial world to develop an alternative force to our own Armed Forces.

As you know, many of these security consultant forces exist, including Aegis Defense Services, Asia Security Group, and Academi, formally Blackwater. And not to mention what's left of the Wagner Group. As a concerned American citizen, I've been building my own private group for some time. I would like to make it available to you, at a reasonable cost, to help police the country during your first term.

We've only met a few times, but I believe you'll find me an eager business partner who shares your ultimate goals for peace and security.

Sincerely,

Armand Ramsey

Robinson dropped the letter on her desk, took off her glasses, and rubbed her tired eyes. Extortion? Is that what this is? A classic protection racket?

She knew Ramsey's reputation well. A megalomaniacal financier who represented everything wrong with Wall Street, and frankly, with the Republican Party. He had long advocated a breaking apart of the West and Midwest from the elites on the East Coast and was a character of great renown on the conservative cable channels, even if he never gave interviews.

What could he possibly gain from working with the federal government to build a second armed force, besides money? Which he didn't need. She thought of the paramilitary groups that operated in exchange for natural resources in traditional hot spots such as Haiti, Syria, and even Afghanistan. But those all took advantage of countries without effective governments.

Of course, she'd have to pass this message off to McHenry and his team, including the FBI and CIA. He would know that. If he was behind the attacks, as his message implied, it would be tantamount to handing himself over.

Robinson stared up at the fog fingers, now tightly grasping the upper-hill homes of Sausalito. She struggled to see a motive. The sun was just beginning to set over Mount Tam when it hit her like a freight train.

She called her security team. "How did this message come in, Warren?"

"Standard encrypted phone text," Madam President-Elect. "We can't trace it, but it does say who it's from."

"Maybe," Robinson said to herself. "Get me the President."

Chapter 4

Hoken walked into the courtyard of her Lincoln Park apartment complex, past the cheap hedges growing from piles of wet, creeping midwestern mud. She walked up to her second-floor flat, pushed through the door, and collapsed on the couch. Something was troubling her.

As news of a second attack, this time in California, played on her computer, she kept thinking about Willis and the Cubs hat. The missing Glock as well. He could have lost it anywhere, but something wasn't right. The blood was on the outside of the cap, staining the stitched-red C. As if it had spattered.

She thought about what his family had said. Cubs fan. Vietnam. Union. NRA. Nothing out of the ordinary in middle America. But something was wrong. She looked him up on Google. Nothing.

What was the plastics factory? They hadn't given a name. She looked up plastics factories within a few "L" stops of his house. There was an American Plastics factory in Harwood Heights, out by the American Metal Manufacturing plant. Different company, owned by a West Coast venture capital firm.

She knew that the company had consistently had labor problems, so she dug a little deeper. There were indeed union protests in the last few months outside the gates, complete with police and tear gas and the usual stuff. No mention of Willis.

She grabbed her bag and hopped a taxi over to Rose's.

Rose's Tavern was a classic North Chicago sports tavern. A dirty window and pea-green door led into a dark long room, lined with dirt-encrusted men on faux-leather, red barstools, passing the afternoon lying to each other about their past and watching Bears highlights on SportsLine.

A hairy bartender in a Bulls cap looked her up and down as she approached the nearest corner, threw a dirty rag over his gray flannel, shirt shoulder, and walked over.

"What-cha having?" he said.

"Small diet coke, thanks."

Hoken met the stares of the regulars. She knew all their stories. Growing up in the UP, she was well acquainted with those looks of desperation. The relaxed feeling of sitting among people who didn't care what you did or who you were, as long as you were good for a little small talk about sports or a dirty joke.

The bartender, Eric, set her soda down on a paper napkin and looked at her for payment. She slipped him a ten and told him to keep it.

"Thanks, lady," he said.

"I have a question though."

He looked at her suspiciously, wondering which of his customers was her ex-boyfriend or lost husband.

"I'm working with the family of Pearson Willis."

Heads jerked.

"Lawyer?" someone said.

"Journalist. WBBM."

No response. Drinks to lips all around.

"The family is concerned this is more than an accidental shooting. They found blood in his bedroom on his clothes," she said, leaving out the cap.

"Peers was a good guy, that's all I'll say," a skinny, black scotch and water with white stubble and a Peterbilt truck shirt volunteered. "Didn't deserve to end up like that. Outside a church too. Shiiit."

The bartender glared at him, then Hoken.

"Family said he had friends here," she said. "Friends who might want to help."

"Lady, people come here to get away from their troubles, not discuss them," Eric said, wiping sweat from his upper lip with the dirty rag.

"Thanks, man," said another customer down the middle of the bar, crushing the last of a draft Old Style and tossing a fistful of crumpled dollars. He picked up a cane and limped past the others and Hoken without even looking at her.

Someone put Frank Sinatra on the jukebox, drowning out any hope of hearing about the Bears' dwindling playoff hopes or any more discussion about Pearson Willis.

"Don't get us wrong," we all loved Peers," said a third regular, a younger man unsuccessfully trying to fill out a Ron Santo jersey. "He was great entertainment during a Cubs game. Knew all the stats and nobody could beat him in an argument about team history. Also, after enough whiskey, he made a great drunk Harry Caray impression. But he never talked about much else."

Hoken picked up her soda and walked down the bar behind the men and one woman. The classic combination of ancient beer signs, sports pennants, and animal photos from whatever warehouse decorated all dive bars. Nervous eyes followed her ass, then shifted forward as she turned.

She walked back to the bar and wrote something on a napkin. "My number at work. Just in case," she said and slid it across to Eric.

As she walked out, he snatched it and threw it away.

Hoken reached for her glasses as she left Rose's. Nothing more distressing than leaving a comfortable dark bar into the blinding sunlight of a day still going on strong without you.

As she adjusted to the glare, she noticed the man with the cane across the street, looking at her. He turned and walked around the corner. She followed.

Halfway down the block, she saw him sitting on a stoop, next to a tobacco shop, smoking.

"A bar like that is no place to discuss business," he said in a breath of smoke. "I worked with Peers. One of the greats. Didn't know his family but I imagined they'd be asking questions."

Hoken simply nodded and resisted the temptation to sit down or take out her notebook. Sometimes the slightest movement threw them off their track.

"Only thing I can guess, assuming it wasn't an accident like half the other shootings in this shit town, is that he pissed off some folks across town," he said, laying his cane across his lap.

"What folks?"

He blew another cloud. "Peers was the money man for our union. Reported into a larger operation down in Pullman. Boss by the name of Ken Sadowski," he said, looking both ways down the street. "Peers was an emotional guy. Cubs fan, you know the type. Sometimes he'd fly off the cuff. Was pissed the money he raised from dues didn't come back to his boys in kind. Thought some of it was going elsewhere, but that's all I know.

He was the kind of guy who would tell you to your face if he was unhappy though. Maybe he told the wrong guy."

Hoken hadn't heard of Sadowski, but he would be easy enough to look up.

"If I hear anything else, how can I contact you? What's your name?"

He blew one more cloud, then pushed himself up on his cane and turned back. "Boys at Rose's call me CJ. That's all I got, babe." And he walked away.

***

Ramsey took a last drag of a Marlboro Light and tossed it out his car window. He sat across the street from the Willis' house on W. Fletcher. Ramsey hated Wrigleyville. He was a White Sox fan, delivered by his dad while growing up on the South Side, and he hated the rowdy smugness Cubs fans exhibited, pretty much the world over. Outside of Chicago, being a Cubs fan was like being a Dallas Cowboys fan in the 1970s. The loveable losers had become a marketing machine.

The FBI had turned up an interesting connection between the Ingram Mac10s connected to the drones and a spate of local killings using the machine pistols in Chicago in the last four months. Chicago Police Department Chief Ted Holland was brought in and instructed Ramsey to run background checks on some three dozen of the guns used in local killings, many of them random.

While waiting for the results, Ramsey drove over to the Willis' house. He had given it several hours in hopes that reporter had left, but was still not looking forward to another family-led goose chase.

Juno was bound to the cracked, brown door when Ramsey knocked, causing a ruckus as Keisha grabbed him and handed him to Uncle Darrell.

"Hello, Miss Willis, Lt. Ramsey again."

"I remember, hello."

"A reporter called me and said you found something unusual in your dad's room."

"I didn't think we'd see you, but thanks for coming. Yes, his favorite Cubs hat, spattered in blood. He wasn't wearing it when he was shot, so something must have happened beforehand."

"May I see it?"

Keisha walked him into the living room and took the hat off a towel on the mantle. "The blood is all on the outside, which we thought was weird."

"Could be from anything, but I'm happy to have it tested," Ramsey said. "Can I bring it with me?"

"Sure, but we want it back, clean if you can. We want to keep it as a memory."

"I'll see what I can do. By the way, I know I asked you before if your dad had any enemies. Does this hat trigger anything?"

"Not really," she said. "He would wear it to and from work, and always on the weekends, except for church. He never wore it in church. And they didn't let him wear it with his work uniform."

"Your father was active in the union at work, right? I seem to remember a few labor disputes in the headlines. Maybe as part of some extra-curricular activity?"

"He didn't really discuss that stuff with us," said Keisha.

Darrell shifted uncomfortably in the easy chair. "He did have a beef with one of his superiors. A guy named Sadowski. Pretty sure it was over money, as that's the only thing that ever-got Pearson riled. Not sure who owed who. But I seemed to remember it was union-related."

Ramsey noted the name in his phone. Chicago was infamous for its corruption, and nowhere was it worse than in local union politics. The legendary machines of former Mayor Richard Daley, and then his sons, Richard and William, literally financed their parties on union money. Might as well have said Willis was fighting with Mexican drug cartels.

Still, a lead was a lead. He stood up to go and gingerly grasped the lid of the Cubs hat with two fingers. "Thanks, I'll make sure you get it back."

Outside in his black Dodge Charger, Ramsey tossed the hat roughly into the back seat. His phone was buzzing. Agent Bledsoe at the lab had connected a couple dozen of the guns to a single shop on the South Side, owned and operated by several men, whose names meant nothing. Williams, Daniels, Sadowski... wait, Sadowski?

"What's the full name?"

"Kenneth Sadowski," Bledsoe said. "Address in Pullman."

Ramsey stuck his glasses on and stared hard at his phone screen. Wait for it. Wait for it. There, one of the guns was used in the Willis shooting.

"Now we're getting somewhere," he said to himself, lighting another smoke and pointing his car toward Rogers Park.

***

Ken Sadowski had a low profile in local Chicago politics, but a large shadow. Few people on the wrong side of him wanted to hear his wet-gravel voice, or worse, feel his calloused hands on their shoulders. He was brilliant at collections, though, and many of the local union shops used him to keep the money coming in.

Of course, once it got to Sadowski, nobody was quite sure where it went. Everybody seemed to get paid though, and aside from the Italian steaks and chops at Gene and Georgetti's he couldn't resist several times a week, Sadowski lived below the radar.

He had money stashed in dozens of bars, garages, and seedy weapons shops or shooting ranges on the South Side, and it was to the one called "Louie's Bar and Shot" on Pullman Crossing, behind the Whole Foods distribution center, that he walked into the back of this morning.

An attendant had said a woman who had asked for him earlier, before opening, and said she'd come back, was now outside. Sadowski cracked the office door open and looked out at her across the bar. Skinny jeans and Ray-bans crossed at the belt outed her clumsy attempts to fit in the neighborhood with a baseball hat and sweatshirt. He'd talk to her, but he'd bring his friend just in case.

Sadowski slipped the Beretta into the small of his back and walked out to greet Hoken, a crusty hand extended over the bar.

"What can I do for you, honey?"

"Hoken, Lindsey Hoken, WBBM. I'm investigating the death of a member of a union at a plastics factory on the North Side and your name came up."

"I don't go to the North Side, ma'am. Much less to a plastics factory. But I do know that this is not the type of neighborhood a pretty little bird like you should be walking around in asking questions."

Hoken's blue-green eyes narrowed as she absorbed the misogyny. It was always the same.

"They said you collect the money for most of the unions in this town."

"I have relationships with some unions and have helped them invest in some cases. But that's about all, cutie," he said, turning up the pressure and stepping around the bar.

"Mr. Sadowski, I'm a reporter. It's not hard to look you up and speculate that you do a lot more then help them invest. Now I'm not here to write about you. I want to know if you knew Pearson Willis."

"Doesn't ring a bell. Drink?

"Too early. I see from the sign on the wall you're a proud NRA member. He was too. Ring anything there?"

"My patience," he said, approaching her. "And my blood pressure. Perhaps you could help," grasping her shoulders in those hands.

Hoken twisted but she was in a vice. She threw out a knee but he deflected, spun her around, and reached up her shirt from behind, grabbing her left breast. "No, goddam it," Hoken struggled.

"Nobody can hear you, missy. Nor will they believe you're anything but a whore looking for some extra money down here."

"Actually, I heard," said Ramsey, suddenly in the door.

Sadowski spun Hoken in front of him, still grabbing her breast. With his other hand, he swung his Berretta around at Ramsey, who stood there passively. "Get the fuck out of here."

Hoken used the tiny bit of freedom from one of the hand vices to twist enough to back kick into Sadowski's right calf, causing him to swear and release the other hand. She pushed him away as Ramsey swung his pistol up. Both fired at the same time. Sadowski collapsed in a heap, grabbing his left thigh.

"Son of a bitch," he said, as Ramsey grabbed his gun and cuffed him. Hoken breathed hard and reached under her sweatshirt to adjust her bra.

"Where did you come from?"

"You asked me to help."

"What?"

"Lt. Ramsey at your service."

"What are you going to do with this thug," Hoken said, sitting down and grabbing her notebook. She wanted to record everything she could remember about Sadowski, who was sitting quietly on a bar stool, rubbing his leg. Thick, dark eyebrows. The scar below his left ear. Black eyes and nostrils that flared like a bull.

"I can keep this guy a few days for shooting at me, but not much longer if he's as connected as I think he is."

"I am, and you will both be sorry."

A squad car showed up and carted Sadowski away as Ramsey and Hoken walked out toward his car.

"Need a ride?"

"Sure. Back to the newsroom."

Once inside, Hoken glanced at herself in the mirror and turned with her bag in front of her.

"I owe you thanks. Didn't think it would turn that ugly that quickly."

"These guys know no limits when it comes to what they want. They have absolute power in their worlds, and they are used to taking it all. Glad I could help."

"Do you think there is anything there? He doesn't seem smart enough to manage union money, much less invest."

"Don't underestimate these guys," Ramsey said. "All these bars and shops down here wash money as a matter of course. "Why do you think they're open?"

"So, he must have someone he works for, right?"

"I'll get a chance to question him. In the meantime, do me a favor and be careful," he said. "As soon as I hear someone is coming to bail him out, that means the message will be out about what happened. People like this hate reporters even more than cops. At least we can be bought," he said, with a smile and a sideways glance.

Hoken didn't hear him.

She was looking out the window when she saw the drone hovering twenty-five feet overhead.

***

It looked like a small American eagle in a deep dive toward prey. Stiff, resolute, somehow angry. Perhaps a three-foot wing span, if the metal bars that held it together were wings. Hoken didn't recognize the markings, but she recognized they were red, white, and blue. With a black line through them.

On its nose, where the eyes would be, was a camera, and it was pointed right at them. Below it hung a steel harness, perfect for carrying bags, even small crates, or a gun.

It was flying at the exact pace of Ramsey's Charger, as if some sort of guard. But Hoken knew it was streaming them to someone.

"Make a left here," she said.

Ramsey, still waiting for a response to his line, glanced briefly at the woman, shrugged, and turned left. It stayed with them.

"We're being followed," Hoken said.

Ramsey looked in his mirror.

"Not there. Above. A drone."

He leaned over, catching a whiff of Hoken's shoulder-length, black hair, and strained his eyes up. He saw it briefly.

"What is it doing?"

"Nothing. Just letting us know it's there."

A few blocks later, as they turned onto Lake Shore Drive, the drone disappeared.

Ramsey struggled to think. Had Sadowski pressed some sort of button to alert someone? Did the bar have a camera? Likely both.

Now he was interested. Men like Sadowski didn't have that technology at their disposal. He was a Beretta in the belt guy. But somehow, he did, and both Hoken and Ramsey pondered the wider implications as they drove silently back toward WBBM.

Approaching Millennium Park, they were stopped by traffic and a police presence. Hundreds of protesters had gathered, brandishing signs about the right to bear arms. Many of them carried rifles, old muskets, and of course, pistols.

"We need to defend ourselves against a government that would attack its own people from the sky," a leader with a megaphone shouted. "Guns yes, government no."

The attacks in Chicago and Berkeley had touched a national nerve beyond the usual rush to arm after a random shooting. These were coordinated attacks, and as long as there was no perpetrator, it was dangerous not to think it was their own government, the protesters reasoned.

Hoken wondered briefly if the drone had flown away as they neared the protestors. Something like that flying over would trigger a shooting gallery, the way the country felt right now. They turned back toward the river and went up Michigan Avenue.

Chapter 5

Col. Allen Starks snapped off his phone and gazed out at Lake Tahoe. It was a sparkling fall day, and the orange and red leaves of the trees glistened on the still-blue water like Christmas lights.

There was always some issue to deal with. Everything had gone perfect so far and he was five days away from Operation Charlie. The country was in a furor now over guns and self-protection. "Up in arms, a nation challenged," read the banner strap on CNN's twenty-four-hour coverage.

Charlie would ignite the fuse that would send the militias to the streets. In short order, President McHenry would be stupid enough to declare martial law, and then the fun would begin.

The call had come from Wisconsin. "Chicago missed a drop point this morning," the voice on the line had said. "Sadowski didn't show. No reason to worry yet. He's probably at the track."

Starks always worried. He required weekly drops from his managers in forty-five cities to pay for the coming war. One wouldn't kill him, but he wasn't going to let it slip. Everything must be locked down tight before he would give the green light.

"Find that fat fuck and get him up there with the money now," Stark had hissed.

Starks walked out on his deck and looked through his binoculars across Crystal Bay to the Hyatt Lake Tahoe Resort. Last weekend had been a weaker take at the resort's casino, as the attack on the college game in Berkeley had prompted the NCAA to shut down the rest of the games that day. Thankfully, the morning slate had already played. And the NFL was too greedy to stop the Sunday games.

Football season was always prime time in Tahoe, Reno, Vegas, or any place with a casino. The sportsbook came alive. Only March Madness could compare. Security will be massive around the country this coming weekend. That was okay; Charlie was set for Tuesday after everyone had breathed a sigh of relief.

Starks gazed at the lake. It had been a long journey from Fallujah in Iraq when he had laid there with shrapnel in his thigh one morning from a rocket attack, bleeding out in the hot sun while the battle known as Operation Fury raged around him. One of his buddies, Jackknife, finally found him, and he was medevacked back to Kuwait. He spent Christmas, 2004, recovering in a dusty military hospital, listening to football on the Armed Forces Network and grabbing ass with the nurses. He was able to finish out the tour, his second, that spring.

Starks missed combat. He missed the dust and mud; the cacophony of explosions and orders; the general confusion, fear, and adrenaline which fed his inner rage and spurred him to take risks most in his unit would not.

He was a decorated colonel in the 1st Marine Regiment, which did most of the fighting in that battle, one that would go down with Iwo Jima in Marine lore.

He came back to the States ignored, unappreciated, and bitter. As a black man from New Orleans, who had joined the Armed Forces to escape the streets his two older brothers inhabited, Starks felt trapped. Gambling saved him.

A deckhand's job on a riverboat casino introduced him to the world of gambling and organized crime. He worked his way to the tables, then the floor manager, and he learned how to fight in a different world. One focused on money but with the same intrigue, evil, and cruel personalities as in wartime. Starks felt right at home. Appreciated, feared, but this time wealthy.

Starks looked good in a tux on the floor. But he was equally comfortable kneecapping any toughs sent by a competitor to mess with him or his bosses. Over time, he got connected to the mob in Vegas, and was sent to Reno to run operations. There, he began to build his empire.

Starks thrived on the code of the gambling mobs. The sense of loyalty. Like the Marines. And the swift, merciless retribution on those who tested that loyalty. His bosses loved him as few wise guys at that level were black. He was in and out before anyone noticed.

Police were the enemy, and the more he witnessed the horrors inflicted on his fellow blacks by police in Ferguson, Denver, New York, or Minneapolis, the angrier he became.

Starks had never been interested in America's mission in Iraq. Once you're on the ground, it's all about protecting your fellow Marines. "It's us against them, and that means everybody," Jackknife used to say. War was simply semi-regulated gangs of warriors protecting each other while grabbing territory. He was forever linked to the men in his unit, and they to him. Oorah!

Starks was convinced the U.S. government was working against its people, especially the minorities. Blacks. Latinos. Native Americans. The Armed Forces were too invested to change things, so he took it upon himself.

Starting with some of his old buddies from the unit, Jackknife, Cutter, Smiling Sam, and Gunbarrel Billy, Starks created a group of former military men, who then recruited from the ranks of the hundreds of rag tag militias that dot the American Northwest and upper Midwest. Guns, a love of combat, and a hatred for government fed the group as it grew. But unlike others, it was no club. Starks was creating an army. Children of the Light Horse was born.

Chapter 6

Ramsey dropped Hoken off at WBBM and watched her get out of the car. He liked the way her hair hung over her eyes, and the way she swung her shoulders with confidence. This woman wasn't scared of some thug like Sadowski. He probably got off easier with a bullet to the thigh than what she might have done to him. He felt a sense of wanting to protect her; not that she needed it.

She was out of his league anyway. College-educated, professional, and passionate about her work. He was just limping along through the years, trying to stay alive on Chicago's mean streets until he could retire to that fishing cottage near Egg Harbor in Wisconsin that he always admired on his trips there.

He turned the car north up Lake Shore and decided to stop by Willis' plastics plant. The blood on the Cubs cap had come back from the lab and it wasn't his.

The guard at the gate was useless. He said he couldn't enter without a warrant. But a few workers heading out heard him say something about Willis and the union, and they told him most of that stuff was done offsite. Usually at a bar called Rose's Tavern a few blocks away.

Ramsey asked them if they had heard of Willis getting in a fight before he died, and they shook their heads. They didn't want to talk anymore.

Ramsey cracked the door to Rose's and adjusted his eyes. One Windy City dive bar looked just like another, and Rose's fit the picture. He asked the bartender if he knew Willis. Eric rolled his eyes.

"Let me guess, another reporter."

"CPD," Ramsey said, flashing his badge. "Was there a reporter here."

"Yeah, some honey from that radio station. Cute ass. Too many questions."

"Well, I just got one. You have a back room?"

Eric's eyes shifted instinctively to the back.

"Yeah, but it's occupied now. Neighborhood meeting."

"I'll just take a look," Ramsey said, starting to the back.

"Don't you need a warrant or something," Eric said.

"Not if you just let me back," Ramsey said without looking over his shoulder.

He opened the door to a group of middle-aged men in American Plastic's uniforms, drinks in front of them.

"What the hell you want?" one said.

"Sorry guys. Just checking out the space for a party," Ramsey said.

"He's a cop, guys," Eric said. "Just barged in."

"This is just an informal union meeting, officer," another one said.

Ramsey looked around. Normal back-office files, and a few labor signs on the walls. "Pearson Willis used to join these?" he asked.

The men looked at each other.

"He was our boss, but, well you must know if you're a cop."

"Yeah, I'm trying to find his killer. Any ideas?"

They looked at each other again. Shook their heads.

"Didn't think so," Ramsey said. "Look gentlemen, I'm not interested in union politics, or even what little side hustles you got running. "But I arrested a guy named Ken Sadowski this morning and…"

The name shocked the group, and they glanced terrified at one another.

"Seems like you know him."

"Look officer…"

"Ramsey."

"Officer Ramsey, Peers kept union money issues to himself. That's one of the things we got to figure out now he's gone. But he'd run his mouth off once in a while, and it was clear he had a beef with that guy. That's all I know."

"Do you know how that beef might have ended up getting blood all over his favorite Cubs hat?"

The group looked at each other again. All of them knew the cap.

"Protest a few weeks ago. Usual stuff with police and company management. Bit rough. But one guy set Peers off. There was a scuffle and suddenly Peers was on him, hitting him in the face with his hat and fist."

"Who was he? Not union?" said Ramsey, now pulling up a chair and rolling up the sleeves of his wrinkled, white dress shirt.

The men stood up in unison. "This ain't no courtroom, officer. In fact, it's a bit too private," one said, and he started to walk out.

"Not union," another said. "But he was mad at Peers about something. Mad enough to pull a blade and then Peers and Dickie Jones grabbed him and struck it cross his face"

"Just another day at American Plastics," said the fourth man. "Guy got up and ran and we all just kept marching and yelling."

"After that, didn't see Peers in the hat."

Ramsey thought for a minute. Police on the line might have a video of the scuffle. He'd check when he got to the car.

"Guys, I'm much obliged to you." Turning to Eric, he said, "Have a round on the copper," and handed him a twenty and two fives.

"If it helps get justice for Peers, then we're happy to do it. But we'll take the beer."

***

Hoken watched the protests from the newsroom and didn't like what she saw. These were not the Black Lives Matter folks from a few years ago. There were protesters from all races, but they seemed more like the anti-globalization protests from the time of the Great Financial Crisis.

Essentially, they were protesting the way the world worked. But specifically, the world's institutions. And here in the U.S., with a new president about to take over—

a black one—the protests were a throbbing, raw wound from years of inequality, racism, and mostly, elitism. A message was being sent that after two hundred and fifty years, the people wanted a new system.

America had a history of protests, but Hoken knew the most dangerous ones were these types: The French Revolution, the Russian Revolution, the revolutions in South America in the 70s. Revolutions that started on the streets, dissolved into anarchy, and gave rise to a bloody new order, with powerful strongmen seizing control. Napoleon, Stalin, Pinochet.

In just the last two decades, Erdogan in Turkey, Duterte in the Philippines, Orban in Hungary. Vladimir Putin's and Russia's destruction in Ukraine, and above all threats, Xi Jinping in China. Even President Trump had managed to rip apart precious Democratic freedoms during his reign, taking pages from the others and writing new ones for future tyrants.

It wasn't just Chicago. These protests were in seventy-five major cities and in hundreds of smaller towns and country sides. The Guy Fawkes masks of the original protesters had given way to Charlton Heston masks, for the former actor and gun enthusiast forever famous for his remark at an NRA convention that if the government ever came for his gun, they'd have to "pry it from my cold, dead hands."

On the masks, an older Heston, screaming in rage and indignation, is depicted. Completing the uniforms were the great American colors, blazing in their football jerseys. Patriots, Cowboys, Raiders. Tribal violence made for TV.

Threatening but uniquely American. Everyone carried a firearm.

Police had learned the hard way not to engage. To channel and contain the raging crowd as it moved through a city. But if things reached a tipping point, they were allowed to respond with overwhelming force. Hoken hoped the police wouldn't be provoked. She feared a war might start that the government was not prepared to finish.

"What are you thinking? Hoken looked up to see her City Editor, Joan Grantwell.

"Nothing. Just worried about these protests,"

"We've seen worse," said Grantwell, a veteran of Chicago political history, who had worked her way up from the City News Bureau covering cops, to the Sun-Times to WBBM. "After Minneapolis, I thought the whole country would go lawless. Then Covid brought the anti-Asian attacks and smash-and-grab craze, and suddenly we needed police again. Seems nothing has changed."

"I don't know," said Hoken, more to herself. Turning fully to her boss and standing, Hoken flicked her hair over her shoulder and looked at her notebook. "I might have something on this Pearson case. He was a union leader over at American Plastics and got in some money spat with the local mob.

Hoken didn't mention her meeting with Sadowski or how Ramsey had saved her.

"Okay, keep pulling the threads," said Grantwell. "Especially with these local crime bosses, it almost always leads somewhere."

Hoken sat back down and turned to her computer. An email from Ramsey.

"I may have something for you, off the record, of course."

"Of course, let's hear it."

"Not on this. Can you meet me after work? Gibson's?"

"What is this, some sort of date?" Hoken sighed. Here we go again.

"No, I'm just thirsty. See you at seven-thirty pm."

Hoken clicked off and idly browsed through Google for anything on Sadowski. He certainly kept a low profile. Nothing. A few arrests years ago. Mug shots. Group photo at Arlington Race Track.

Wait, in the winner's circle. She looked again. There he was standing with three other guys in the winner's circle four years ago with a horse named Public Enemy. Apt, she smirked. The other guys, listed as co-owners, were named Vincent Giacobbe, Peter Miller, and Ryan Delaney. She ran them all through Google first. Not much. Then her police files.

Hoken sat straight up. Suddenly she needed to talk to Ramsey beyond just shooting the shit over a gin and tonic.

***

Army Johnson looked at his watch. The timing was perfect. The bait had been set and Reno was ready.

"This will be the tipping point," he told Starks while tying his sneakers for a jog. Johnson was a fitness buff and an avid runner. He had run the Boston Marathon a few years back and had marveled at the beauty of the historic city he was about to wreak havoc on. "A gut punch to the heart of the American story."

"Yeah, some story," Starks replied. Johnson grimaced as he looked at his silver and gold burner phone, the colors of his beloved Colorado Buffaloes. He had met the former Marine through one of his political connections in Washington D.C., who had told him about the Children of the White Horse. He considered him another embittered combat veteran just like his political friend, but he admired his ability to control a vast army. He would need them both in the coming days.

"Where are we with Jackknife," Johnson asked about the friend.

"He and I got it covered. Don't you worry. You and your money are well hidden here," Starks said. "Our inventory at the casino is all cash, you know."

Starks wasn't a big fan of Johnson. He admired how he had clawed his way up, but he wasn't a leader of men, such as Starks fancied himself. Still, he was financing this war, and Starks would take care of any personality issues later.

"Get ready for Operation Tea Party," he said and signed off.

Chapter 7

The protests on Boston Common had been uncommonly quiet for the last several days, compared to the rest of the country. The city, known for its racist past and fierce fighting during the school busing crisis of the early 70s, was usually quick to jump on a cause – any cause, as long as it was liberal enough.

These protests were different, though. The Brady shirts made everything feel like another Super Bowl victory parade, but the Heston masks underscored a darker theme. Boston's police department, having shut down the city to capture the Boston Marathon terrorists several years ago, was the toughest in the country. But now they were on the back foot.

Officer Brian Connolly walked across the Public Garden across the street with eyes darting from side to side. At thirty years old, he was accustomed to seeing people carrying firearms in the streets. But for most of his career, he had assumed he was the target, so he always kept his gun holster unstrapped, against regulations.

"Good afternoon, officer," a young couple said from a nearby bench, as their two-year-old stumbled among the famous Make Way for Ducklings statues. Connolly smiled. He thought of the police officer in the book, stopping traffic to let the ducks cross a busy street. They don't make them like that anymore.

Nobody knew where the Chicago and Berkeley attacks came from, but a lot of spin was pointing to the authorities. Sick of the years of unrelenting gun violence across the country, speculation that President-Elect Robinson was coming to clean things up made both sides nervous.

It gave a perfect opportunity to someone or some group to exploit the situation by lighting the tinderbox of American government hatred. As police followed orders to hold back, many protests had been on the verge of turning into mayhem. But in Boston, they had been relatively peaceful. The police were stubbornly respected. Until now.

Marie Wilson was wearing the purple and white of her Emerson University and holding a sign saying "We won't take it anymore," which could have been used in just about any protest throughout history. But she marched and chanted with the intensity of a college student wanting to change the world, raising her hoarse voice in unison with the crowd.

She looked at her watch and pointed her sign at a tall, hairy guy next to her. "I got to go. Meeting some folks for a concert on the Esplanade. See you tomorrow."

Wilson left the protests and walked down Charles Street carrying her sign, past the packed Sevens Pub, where college students waited in line to play darts and quaff Harpoon lager from pint glasses off the polished wood bar. The Sevens was the original inspiration for the old TV show "Cheers," which her mom and dad had made her watch once. She didn't understand the appeal.

She headed toward the bandshell on the Esplanade, where she was going to listen to some jazz music and get high with a couple of friends out by the Charles River. It was windy that afternoon and Wilson was staring out at the normally placid waters to admire the whitecaps on the river when she saw them.

They looked like a swarm of locusts coming straight down the river from the Harvard boathouse. Wilson did a double-take, then watched dumbfounded for several seconds trying to make out what they were. By the time she realized, it was too late. Wilson dropped the sign and ran screaming toward the street, pointing behind her as tourists, students, and jazz fans looked up from their blankets in a haze of smoke.

The drones were on them in a heartbeat, moving with perfect synchronized formation, like an angry pterodactyl, swooping up, and launching downward. Except these were spraying bullets. Wilson caught one in the back of the thigh and sprawled into the concrete bike path near the road, scraping her face.

She looked up and saw a man's body perfectly splayed out beside her, a hole in the back of his head. She started crawling, but the great, black bird of fire had already passed, up and over the T tracks and across the lower part of Beacon Hill, firing down on Charles Street and the lines outside the Sevens.

Blood spattered on storefront windows as tourists and shoppers caught unaware went down like bowling pins before the swooping drones. Cars slammed into each other as drivers ducked down to avoid bullets shattering windshields.

Police across the country had been instructed to watch for such an attack, but the signals had been jammed and by the time officers on the ground had called it in, the drones were hitting Boston Common's lower lawns and yanking left in unison up toward the State House.

Connolly was standing at the corner of Charles and Beacon when he saw them ripping down Charles Street, right toward him. He dove behind one of the park gates as the drones sped past and made a slight left toward the Common.

Bodies fell and protesters ran. Some kneeled on the ground and started firing wildly into the sky, spraying each other and nearby buildings with gunshots. A seven-year-old boy in the front of one of the swan boats in the Public Garden about a quarter mile away from Connolly took a bullet to the side of the head and tumbled into the water, his mother screaming as she tumbled in after him.

Bullets pounded the pavement walkways leading up to the State House, fifty feet across, and mowing down bodies like a great, black wave. As the drones approached the State House, with its statues of Daniel Webster and John F. Kennedy outside, they suddenly broke into two formations and sliced straight into the sky, sparing the statues and one of the enduring historical symbols of American government.

Witnesses said it almost looked like the finale of Boston's famed July 4th fireworks as they shot into the sky, firing above and beyond the building. But not one bullet hit it.

Within minutes they were gone. Soaring along the waves of the Charles River toward Boston Harbor and out to sea. Police and ambulances descended on the scene of horror, the third in a week in the U.S. This time, however, they were met with more bullets.

Connolly saw it first. As he began to cross the street toward the Common, a bullet whizzed past his shoulder. Another pocked the pavement three feet to his left. He jumped back behind the gate.

"Officer under fire," he shouted into his shoulder receiver. "Protesters firing at everything that moves. Proceed with caution."

Armed protesters began firing at the police as they arrived, screaming obscenities and starting running battles across the city as the mood of the crowd turned against the authorities. A few blocks away, toward Emerson, in what used to be called the Combat Zone, armed students fired at police from behind cars. Social media hummed with videos of the drones soaring above the State House, with accusations that it had been spared because it had coordinated the attacks.

Wilson, lying at the Esplanade holding her leg, watched in horror as arriving paramedics came under fire.

The great conspiracy theory now hung with blood. Was the government indeed attacking its own people? Had this come from the President? Or worse, the President-Elect, to justify her hardcore, anti-Second Amendment position.

In the cradle of liberty, where two hundred fifty years earlier, regulated militias fought off the British and sparked the War of Independence, they wanted answers. And they went for their guns.

***

Neil Young's song 'Ohio' from 1970, which is about the Ohio National Guard shooting four college students from Kent State during protests, was suddenly the No. 1 song on Spotify

An unmistakable shift had happened. One of those shifts that occurs when competing protests—guns, Black Lives Matter, yellow vests, Trans Lives Matter, even Me Too—suddenly come together with a common enemy: The State.

McHenry struggled with this in the Oval Office as his phone rang. He did not want this to be his legacy.

"President-Elect Robinson on the line," his aide said. "Put her through."

"Mr. President. Tom. What's going on?"

"We're at war, Ginny. And we don't even know who with."

"You got my message," she said.

"Yes, my team is looking at Army. That bastard has always been an opportunist, but we've no evidence that connects him to these things other than his threat."

"Isn't that enough to bring him in or scare the shit out of him?" she said. "I've been thinking about his message.

He's daring us to turn him down because he knows the people are turning against us."

"We are going to talk with him, but without evidence, he's just offering to help," McHenry replied.

"What do you know? I've been gradually brought in on classified information, but I need to know everything now. I take over in two months."

"And until then I'm still the president, Ginny. I'm sorry. Adding you and your team to this info exposes us even more to whoever is behind it."

"Just tell me," she sighed. "Why we can't track down these fucking drones."

"The problem is in the breakup. As long as they are a coordinated squadron, we can track them on radar, or if they are too low, using wireless tracking and motion sensors," he said.

"But that is only for the few minutes it takes them to execute the attack. Before we can scramble aircraft or get a bead on where they are going, they scatter in a hundred different directions. Some, we think, simply drop from the sky. Some go east. Some west. Others seem even to have the capacity to jam the motion sensors.

"It's as if they are a band of wild Indians, scattering back into the forest after the attack, making it impossible for an army to follow them, Ginny."

"Funny, that's how our early militias learned to fight the British," she said.

"Mmm," said McHenry, who wasn't listening. "If we could just get our hands on one, we could probably reverse engineer it pretty quickly, but so far no luck. The video we've isolated and enlarged makes them look like American Eagles, painted white on the front and stretched out, with huge wingspan and claws holding the guns. We even think some of the guns are equipped with silencers to make them even harder to detect with sounding radar."

"You're telling me we haven't found even one of these things?" said Robinson. "When are you planning to bring me in on this?" she raised her voice.

"Soon, Ginny. Hang in there. This will be your issue soon enough."

"I'm not sure you have that much time, Tom," she said as she hung up.

McHenry leaned back in his chair and gazed out the window at the Washington Monument. She was right. In less than a week, he had been defeated in an election and lost control of the country. The protesters had now turned deadly, and this third attack exposed the limited ability of local police and government to control them. He had to consider martial law.

Homeland Security Chief Robert Pastor came in as McHenry was lost in thought.

"Sir, we have more on Army Johnson," he said.

McHenry looked up.

"It's not much but maybe something to go on," Pastor said. "He seldom strays far from his beloved Colorado, but he makes exceptions for marathons. He's a running nut. Boston, New York, London, Paris, even Moscow."

"Moscow?" McHenry was interested.

"Yes, Moscow. Seems he was there just two months ago, in late September. Finished in three hours forty-seven minutes. He then spent another three days there, mostly holed up at the Ritz-Carlton. No word on who he met, but I've asked our team there to sniff around some more."

"Interesting. Thanks, Bob. I thought this could be Russians. Those fuckers have been causing trouble ever since Crimea. Don't they have enough problems in Ukraine?"

"What does Nikki think?" he said, referencing CIA chief Nikki Forrester.

"I'm meeting with her later," Pastor said. "We know the Russians never miss a chance to cause chaos here, if only to distract us from their operations in Europe. And if you remember, they tested kamikaze drones in Ukraine. Those were essentially tiny guided missiles, but they did have enough AI programmed into them to make target decisions based on pre-selected objectives. That was a decade ago."

"Yeah, I remember. Hey, is Army a gun nut, Bob?" Any chance he wants to sow dissent against us like some of these whackos are saying on Facebook?"

"No, he's not. Other than being a megalomaniac and greedy bastard, he lives a clean life. No booze. No smoking. And he's on the record as hating guns. So maybe his entreaties are real?"

"Fuck that, keep digging," McHenry said.

Pastor stared at McHenry for a long moment, then turned and left as McHenry stared out the window at the Rose Garden. *Not since President Donald Trump had pushed the country to the brink of anarchy a decade before had it been so close*, he thought. *We can't stop the attacks.*

People think it's us. Maybe we just fulfill those theories if only to protect them. And us, he thought.

McHenry grunted. Retirement on his Beaver Creek ranch had seemed so close. Now he didn't even know if he would get that far before losing the democracy. He had to find out who was behind it. And above all, prevent it from happening again. It might already be too late.

McHenry rose and shuffled toward the door to the conference room for his emergency cabinet meeting. He needed to know what Armand Johnson knew. Right away.

Chapter 8

Randy Bob Chatham peered through the crosshairs of his Colt AR-15 Sporter Carbine and gently squeezed the trigger.

Fifty yards away, a target lit up. Seven out of ten in the bullseye. *Not bad*, he thought as he stood up in the desert night and ambled back toward the trailer his militia used for a training headquarters.

The fifty-four-year-old Carson City native and his troop, Black Dawn, were keeping a low profile in the days after the Berkeley attack. The drones began their maneuvers just a mile south of here in an abandoned airstrip. Randy, known as Rambo by his friends and family from his favorite movie as a boy, and Black Dawn had guarded the airfield in the forty-eight hours leading up to the launch of the operation.

They didn't know where the drones were going until they heard of the attack. But Randy knew the orders had come directly from Reno, so he knew it was going to be a big one. A few drones returned. Just enough to not attract attention. The rest had scattered through the Central Valley near Sacramento.

Randy eased his considerable frame into an easy chair and popped open a can of Sierra Nevada. He looked at the three men in the trailer that night and thought about the excitement of the last few years. Randy had started Black Dawn after breaking away from the Battle Born Patriots, one of the better-known unlawful militias in Northern Nevada.

He never liked their internal politics, and frankly, thought they were a bit squeamish in their operative plans. Randy wanted to fight. He had wanted to all his life, but especially since a bad knee had kept him from serving in the army. He had been in the militias all his adult life instead, taking part in two of the three Sagebrush Rebellions, which flared up in the 70s, 90s, and 00s every time the federal government got too pushy. Environmental laws and gun regulations infuriated him. He was a warrior, and he was prepared to defend Nevada from any encroachment, East or West.

Black Dawn had fifty men in it, many of them older like Randy. They had been contacted months ago by an old colonel at one of the gun shows in Reno. He liked the man, even though he was black. The colonel treated Randy like the military man he was, speaking in crisp, no-nonsense bursts like the sound of his carbine.

He called his army Children of the Light Horse, which Randy never understood but was happy to accept as long as he could keep Black Dawn for his team. Like in all tribal or sports allegiances, names were important to these men. Starks preferred it that way too. It kept the size of his ultimate command a secret.

The colonel told Randy to call him by his code name, Starfucker. He said the day of freedom was coming, and that he needed men like Randy and his troops to help save the Union from federal soldiers. He kept the troops on their toes with a multitude of demands, from the weekly cash drops to training maneuvers like this one, to the three or four operations they had now taken part in. He knew the big one was near, as the old colonel had ordered him and his troops to be on red alert throughout the upcoming holidays, and to man the training facility 24/7.

Randy expected the colonel and whoever he worked with were behind the attack in Chicago, but he didn't know. And Starks didn't answer questions. He just gave orders. As far as Randy was concerned, as long as he and his team had a mission, they didn't need to ask questions.

Randy had killed before. Black Dawn demanded at least two kills on your record just to apply. A cop in Carson City. A state EPA official outside of Vegas. But he lusted for more. He wanted a battle. As he guzzled his beer and went for another, he thought about the pleasure of shooting at people who deserved it.

***

Johnson could only laugh as Starks relayed the details of the Boston attack on a secure phone line.

"And then the protesters brought out their own guns and started shooting at the police," Starks said.

"It's almost too easy," Johnson said. "I just got a message from the President. By now he's heard of our offer to Robinson and should be in a fine lather."

"Wait 'til he sees the team we got," Starks said.

"About that, Allen. I know you've got a helluva group built up, but I'm going to need something more. Securing the perimeter is one thing, but we'll need international significance too. I've started talking with Kip Reed at Secura about helping out. We'll need to quickly infiltrate and seize control of overseas forces once we get the green light. Iraq, Germany, Venezuela, Taiwan."

Starks said nothing. He knew the guys at Secura. Second-rate pussies as far as he was concerned. How could his team control the U.S. if someone else had the rest of the world? Besides, that's not what he wanted.

"Once we get the go from McHenry, and Robinson for that matter, we can be ready for a seamless security transfer before Inauguration Day.

"This is the critical moment, Allen. We need the old warmonger to go martial before Robinson takes over. He's got to be considering it, given Boston. But we need to keep the pressure on. The protests are building but we don't have long. If no decision by the end of the week, we'll need to move Operation Pigskin up a few weeks, possibly to Thanksgiving."

Starks thought about the logistics of a multi-city attack on Thanksgiving Day or Black Friday, vs mid-December during a football Sunday filled with holiday shoppers. He knew where to strike, but the security would be formidable. He told Johnson he'd have a plan for him in forty-eight hours.

Johnson hung up to get back to McHenry. Starks poured himself a drink and considered his options. This was now the point in the mission where the rubber hit the road. A defense contract from a new administration was not his goal, as lucrative as it might be.

He took out a hundred-dollar bill and lit it on fire, then used it to light a Cohiba Siglo III, his favorite. Money wasn't his thing. He had plenty. Besides, there was no way McHenry called martial law. It would be the end of the Republic. That was fine, but why give the Feds the upper hand?

Thanksgiving weekend it would be. He flicked on his laptop, logged in with his ten-digit code, and called up the plans for Operation Pigskin. Right out of the old 70s movie Black Sunday, with Robert Shaw, but this time it would work.

***

"Mr. President, you've got to do something to stop this senseless carnage," Johnson said. "I'm getting killed in the markets and as the dollar plunges, our collective image declines on the world stage by the day.

"We're prepared to step in the hour you call martial law," he said. "It will take some weeks to do the handover, but until then my troops will be happy to assist the U.S. Army as it secures the country. We'll need a foreign policy position too."

"Army, I don't know what kind of fucked-up air you're breathing out there in cow country, but I am NOT calling martial law. The country isn't ready for it. This isn't Kent State. It's every goddamn city in the U.S."

Johnson paused and glared at the silver and gold phone in his right hand.

"Look, the way I see it you've got a bit less than ten weeks to get this country to calm down. Get Ginny in place, and then you're out here in fucking cow country with me at Beaver Creek. That land is going to skyrocket under a lockdown, and you'll be the hero who saved the Republic. It's certainly not unprecedented in the world. Other leaders use it all the time."

"I'm not other leaders. This is the United Fucking States of America. We don't shoot our people."

"Could've fooled me," Johnson shot back.

"Listen, you fucking bloodsucker, I'm sure you've got this whole thing hedged in every direction and up everybody's ass to make more money for you and your friends. What I want to know is which one of you is behind it?"

"Come on, Tom, of course, I'm betting it, but I'm not behind it. This country has been good to me. What do I have to gain? I'm sure you've bugged me straight up the ass, but you haven't found anything because I'm not the guy. Think of some other enemies. What about those frat-boy tech fuckers? They would love to get the whole country wired into their goddamn platforms. Imagine what the Russians could have done with those back during the Revolution."

"Don't give me that shit. Someone's the mastermind, and it's always a money thing. I'll just say if it is you, then I'll make sure you don't live to see Christmas," McHenry said. "We've got tracers on a couple of those drones," he bluffed. "Should know in a matter of days."

"Well, let me know when you find out so I can buy the dollar," said Johnson, not biting.

McHenry hung up. He buzzed his secretary to get Homeland Security and Pastor back on the line. "They had to track those drones."

Chapter 9

Hoken walked into the crowded bar at Gibson's and looked for Ramsey. She was wearing a white turtleneck sweater with black jeans, knee-high, brown leather boots, and a matching suede windbreaker. It was starting to get colder in Chicago.

Ramsey was at the corner of a crowded bar, but had saved a seat for her. He was nursing a Jameson's on the rocks. A patchy, brown sport coat, hanging over the side of his chair, illustrated his clumsy attempt to dress up for the meeting. Otherwise, his usual white shirt, sleeves rolled up, and black jeans. Hoken sat down and ordered a vodka tonic, one ice rock, and just a splash.

"Haven't been here in years," she mused, looking around at the tourists and businessmen. "Still popular, I see."

Yeah, but you can always find a spot at the bar if you know the bartender, he said, giving a wink to Gino as he poured the vodka.

Hoken smiled politely. She didn't like cops, but this guy had saved her, and he had a dry sense of humor that appealed to her. "Thanks again for earlier," she said.

"No problem. Guys like that can't be left alone with anybody. He's out already, just so you know."

She looked surprised, but then just shrugged. "Maybe he can help lead us to somebody."

"Kenosha," they both said together, then stared at each other in surprise.

"You go first," she said.

"I spoke to a few guys who worked with Pearson Willis. Seems he got into a nasty fight outside the plant a few weeks ago, during a union protest. Some guy said something to him and pulled a knife. Pearson and another guy disarmed him and then beat the shit out of him. Cut him across the face with his own knife. Seems Pearson was hitting him in his bloody face at one point with his hat covering his fist."

Hoken nodded.

"I was able to get footage of the scuffle and ran the guy's image across our database. Low-level scab-buster out of Kenosha. Worked for a bunch of manufacturing companies. Also, a member of one of those militias. You know, the ones preparing for war when the government comes. They march around in a local airfield there."

Hoken nodded again. "Think we have something. That airfield is owned by a guy named Peter Miller, a former Marine in Iraq who flies farm equipment around the country. But also, if you believe the rumors, military equipment for these special contractors. You know, BlackWater and the like? The ones who answer to nobody but always seem to be in the thick of the mayhem."

Ramsey looked at her. He imagined these types of contractors had incredible logistics operations at their disposal to transport equipment and agents at a moment's notice, across the globe. Hoken went on.

"I looked him up after seeing a photo of him with Sadowski at Arlington. Apparently, they share a love for the horses and maybe a small business. He turned up in YOUR police files tied to some illegal horse activity. Turns out he was using drones—drones—to sabotage competing horse farms. Dropping poison, spooking horses, etc. Low-level harassment is common in that business, but someone complained and he got named. Nothing was ever done."

Ramsey winced at the suggestion he had missed something. But he still didn't know what she was talking about.

"So?"

"So" she shot back, banging her glass on the bar. "Ramsey, some mystery guy connected to Sadowski, has an airfield within hundred nautical miles of Grant Park, a bad attitude, and apparently a drone force. Maybe Pearson found something out about how they were running the money, in any one of their operations, and threatened to yack. They send some punk to rough him up or worse, and the punk gets punked. So, they come back again, and this time they don't miss."

Ramsey shook the ice in his scotch.

"Call me Dale," he said, still looking at his drink.

Hoken's grip tightened on her drink, but before she could say anything, he turned to her and put both hands on her shoulders.

"The difference between reporters and detectives, Lindsey, is that all you have to do is connect the dots. I have to prove it. But I sure do like where you're going with this."

Hoken didn't know whether to slug him or hug him. In his smug, chauvinistic way, he had actually admitted that she beat him to the scoop. Kind of cute, but he was a bit old, and too Chicago for her. She wanted to be a foreign correspondent, and she planned her relationships with that in mind.

"I'll go back and see if I can draw a line from this goon to Miller's operation," he said. "What's it called?"

"Whispering Dawn Stables is the horse farm outside of Kenosha. Not far from Dawn Field, which he also owns."

Hoken brushed back her hair again. It wasn't that long, just a move she sometimes made when she was nervous around someone. She smiled.

"I'd love to break this one open. That Boston attack makes three in the last week. That's what we in my business call a trend. There is another one coming. I just can't figure out where. It's not just a local story. But there is certainly a local angle, right there in Kenosha."

"Perhaps," Ramsey said. "Now, how about dinner?"

"Okay, but right here at the bar. I want to see the Blackhawks-Rangers game," she said. Gino slid a couple of bar menus over and refilled their drinks.

***

Starks looked at the plan again. It was perfect. Everything Al-Qaeda had missed years ago after 9/11. With the country in panic mode, it would have been so easy to set off a handful of bombs in different cities. Maybe crash a private plane or two for effect. And send the democracy into a tailspin. But they didn't. Their lust for a big strike, shock and awe as our side had coined, was too great. *They didn't realize they only needed a few more yards*, he thought, as he looked up at Sunday Night Football. *He wouldn't make that mistake.*

The plan called for an attack on seven cities, in seven different ways, and including, in two of them, drone strikes. With the economy effectively de-commissioned by the Thanksgiving holiday, the chaos would be complete. McHenry would have no choice but to institute martial law. With luck, he'd even try to cancel the handoff to Robinson and create a constitutional crisis.

That's when Johnson thought they'd call him. But Johnson was wrong, Starks reasoned. They would simply rely on their own troops. And that's when he and Children of the Light Horse would pounce. He put his Cohiba down and smiled as he dialed Randy Chapman on the phone.

***

Randy snapped his phone shut, turned down the sound on the Raiders game, and stood up with glee. "Men, we're moving out. Let's get everyone together."

The order had finally come. They were deploying to Henderson, about six hours away on the other side of the state, just outside Vegas.

They needed to be there by Thursday. Thanksgiving and family would have to wait. Their country needed them.

He wasn't sure what their role would be. Border protection. Immigrant roundup. But he knew Vegas. One of his comrades had shot up the parking lot of the Mandalay Bay hotel years ago in one of the most heinous active shooter attacks in American history. A music festival was going on, and the shooter picked people off from the window of his hotel room above.

The country was appalled. Randy simply nodded. War was hell, and the government needed to be served notice. Now the time had come.

He gathered the troops together and told them the plans. They would deploy in groups of no more than two trucks each, to avoid detection. They would regroup in Henderson in seventy-two hours, on Wednesday night. A large trailer park had been secured for them. They would have adequate time to get settled and even drill during the night, as long as they kept their silencers on.

One of the men objected. He said he couldn't get away because his day job required him to work Thanksgiving that year. Randy shot him on the spot. Number three. He reflected for a moment on how much easier, even enjoyable it gets to take a life. Then turned to the rest of the group. "Anyone else wants to put themselves ahead of the troop?"

Silence.

Two men were dispatched to bury the body in the desert. The rest returned home to say goodbye to their families and to begin the journey.

Randy knew his wife would be dismayed. Thanksgiving was their favorite holiday. Uncles and cousins from both sides would be there on Thursday. After football, there was a shooting contest in the backyard, which Randy always looked forward to.

Three other members of his family were in the troop. There was nothing he could do about it. They were military men and the call to duty could not be ignored.

Black Dawn was on the move.

Chapter 10

Thanksgiving week began with a nation bloodied but unbowed. Terrorism had never stopped it before, and it wouldn't now. Shoppers prepared for the big sales, leading up to Black Friday. Airports were packed. Companies were shutting down or going to skeletal staffs as workers fled for the country, or home to their families.

No amount of skittishness could wipe the fresh, leafy smell of Fall from the air – on either coast, and especially in the heartland. Thanksgiving in America meant food, family, and football. Lots of each. Freedom too, but that had always seemed a given.

McHenry prepared to pardon the turkey at the White House on Wednesday, but before that, he had an urgent cabinet meeting on Tuesday afternoon. The last full day of work before even his trusted advisors would hit the road.

Intelligence had made some progress on the drones. **Nikki Forrester**, head of the CIA, explained that by tapping into airport tracking systems and wireless data from the big telecom companies, they'd been able to establish that in each of the three attacks, drones traveling in groups of three or fewer had been programmed to converge at specific coordinates only two minutes before they hit their target.

"The timing effectively prevents our tracking systems from issuing a warning in time," Forrester said. "But they did allow for enough tracking to monitor what types of drones they were and what types of arms they carried."

They were indeed Ingram Mac-10 machine pistols, attached to fixed-wing hybrid drones, which were winged drones that looked like planes to some extent but with multi-rotor technology. That enabled them to fly with speed but also stop and hover if needed, the best hybrid of winged drones and multi-rotors.

Tens of thousands of these types of drones existed, Forrester explained, under at least a dozen brands. Investigators had reached out to each manufacturer and were combing all sales data, especially within five hundred miles of each of the attacks. Data miners plugged the data into their AI systems to run all sales against purchases of the Ingrams, but so far there were still too many sales points to draw any conclusions.

Homeland Security's Pastor said he expected they'd find the drones were purchased outside the country and made their way in undetected. He had shared the information with Forrester, who nodded her head in agreement. That way if one broke down or got shot down, suspicion would fall on another country. He told the President the path would likely lead to Russia or China, who would easily deny any involvement.

Privately, Forrester wasn't so sure it was the Russians. While they did have extensive experience in drone warfare in Ukraine and beyond that in the Baltics, she'd seen no evidence of these types of coordinated attacks. She thought

Pastor seemed to be pushing the President toward a dangerous accusation that her intelligence operatives could not yet support.

Forrester had come up through foreign service channels. Assignments in Islamabad, Mexico City, and Yemen had prepared her for terror in its worst forms. After three years in London, as an aide to the British ambassador, she understood how diplomatic circles worked as well. She knew that evil existed behind ties and jackets and handshakes just as it did behind guns and bombs.

Pastor, on the other hand, had come straight from the military. McHenry had placed him in Homeland Security without any input from her or her counterpart at the FBI. He was a brilliant tactician, she admitted, but inclined to see everything in black and white, evil vs. good, rather than in the geopolitical shades of gray in which her world operated.

He also exhibited the worst forms of military misogyny and frequently maneuvered to keep her out of his direct access to the President.

McHenry asked how, if the drones crossed over the border, they couldn't be located.

"Why can't we use these wireless transmissions to trace at least one of them to a point of landing or powering down?" he said.

In each of the cases, the drones disappeared over the water after splitting up, where the transmissions were lost, Pastor said. Had they landed on a ship? That would be too easy to trace. They must have returned to shore, but where? Pastor ordered all airports to continue to monitor and send data to his team.

"It's now been two weeks since Chicago, ten days since San Francisco, and six days since Boston," McHenry said. "It's too quiet. I'm worried about the holiday."

"We've got it covered," Pastor said. "We've got extra folks in the airports today and tomorrow. If they hit, it would be one of those days, or maybe Sunday when people are returning home."

"What about the parade in New York?" McHenry said.

"Covered," Pastor replied. Standard rooftop surveillance, airport coverage, and jets prepared to scramble. "My guess is these places are too obvious for whoever this is."

"I need more than guesses, Bob," the president shot back. "What about the protests?"

"We'll be monitoring protests in about 110 cities on Friday," Pastor said. "Combined with the shopping rush, it will be madness on the streets. National Guard on alert for your call-up."

"Okay. What I want are hourly reports, Bob. All through the next six days. Even when I'm sleeping. I want to wake up and immediately know where we are. I want Ginny on speed dial and each and every one of you on call for immediate cabinet meetings, even if you are at the fucking feast table.

"Yes sir," they murmured.

"We need a break here. I've got to have this dealt with before the holidays."

"Yes, sir."

***

Hoken was driving back toward the Upper Michigan Peninsula to see her own family for the holiday early Wednesday afternoon, when she crossed the border into Wisconsin and saw the signs for Kenosha. She always stopped at the Brat Stop for a beer and a brat and a moment of relaxation to enjoy the fact she was back in Wisconsin. Three more hours of driving through cow and cheese country and she'd be back in the U-P.

The Brat Stop hadn't changed for decades. It still had the stage where 70s bands such as Cheap Trick used to play on the Midwest and fairground circuit, and though it had endured several owners and not a few closures, there was always someone who wanted a bar that could seat 700.

Hoken walked in and instinctively went left toward the bars and the stage. She sat down as a friendly bartender walked over and asked her order. "Brat burger, curds, and a tall Spotted Cow," she said without looking at the menu. On the television overhead, talking heads argued about the Thanksgiving Day games on SportsCenter.

She looked back at her phone and then around the bar. The usual photos of Packer players and championship banners, and then some historical photos of areas of Kenosha. Old City Hall. The now-defunct Schlitz Brewery. An old airfield.

Airfield?

"Hi, she said to the bartender. Do you know what that airfield is in the old photo?"

"No, before my time," the bartender said.

"That's old Kenosha Freight," said a guy with a Wisconsin cap and a 'Beer is a food' sweatshirt. "They used to fly farm equipment around the state back in the day. Still do, but it was bought by a guy from Chicago years ago."

"Is that Dawn Field?" Hoken asked.

"Well, that's what it's called now, but that is an old photo. It's a pretty remarkable place now. Very busy. Flights coming in and out day and night. Freight mostly but some fancy jets once in a while. And drones. Lots of drones."

"What do you mean drones?" she asked.

"You know, the little planes. No pilots," he said. Seems they're buzzing all over Kenosha these days. Crazy little things. Surprised they haven't crashed into someone's house with all the chaos on TV lately."

Hoken took a chance. "Maybe there is some military thing going on there. I hear that's where the militia trains."

The beer food guy looked at her strangely. "What you mean, militia?"

"You know, the guys who are preparing for when we need them to protect us," she offered innocently.

"Well, you're looking at one of them, cutie." "Master Sergeant Lombardo at your service. But you can call me Billy."

"Thank you for your service," Hoken shot back, the reporter in her gearing up for the interview. "Is it like what I hear about in Virginia, Quantico, I think."

Billy looked at her again and put down his thirty-two-ounce mug. "That's the FBI. Those are the bad guys. Our boys aren't associated with the government. We're just sworn to protect our homeland when needed."

"Still, pretty cool," Hoken said. "I'd love to come watch you drill at some point. Maybe there is some way I can even participate. Are women allowed in?"

"Not yet," Billy said, reflexively defiant. "But I imagine they'd let you watch at some point, as long as the chief was okay with it."

"The chief?"

"The guy who runs the airfield."

"Ah, you mean Peter Miller," Hoken said, as Billy stopped lifting his mug to his lips a second time. Before he could open his mouth, she said "I met him a few years ago at the track down at Arlington. I ride horses and he owns them, I guess. Nice guy. Said something about a stable and an airfield up here. I didn't know this was the one until you helped me connect the dots."

"Well, I don't know him that well," said Billy, moving a stool closer to her and learning in, beer breath forward. "But I know he's there this week for the holiday. Lots of activity there, especially with the drones. We had Saturday's marching delayed and next Saturday too. So, something going on. The whole place is locked down. Probably flying in friends for the Wisconsin game Saturday in Madison."

Hoken looked down at her beer as her brat burger arrived. She should tell Ramsey—uh, Dale—something was going on. On her way out, she swung by Dawn Field just to take a look. Locked up with an armed guard at the gate, she drove around the back fence and parked and got out. Looked up and down the road and once satisfied she was alone, she walked over to the fence.

She grabbed hold of the wire meshing and peered inside. Just another airfield, as far as she could tell. A couple of freight planes over by the hangar. A nice-looking private jet over by what looked like a small terminal. Some sort of obstacle course in the distance, maybe where they trained. Lots of people in the distance running around, but nobody was near her.

She turned to walk back to the car and there it was, hanging in front of her silently about fifteen feet off the ground, a long machine rifle barrel aimed right at her head. "What are you doing?" it said menacingly. Or rather, a voice wired in said.

Hoken drew a breath. The thing looked like a giant hornet, or worse, an angry eagle. She remembered, just like the one flying alongside Ramsey's—Dale's—car the other day. She didn't know how to respond.

"Don't move," it said.

She stood there for three minutes, then decided to try her luck. She stepped to the left. The rifle barrel made a clicking noise as if cocking to fire. She froze again. Then reached slowly for her phone. It fired into the ground beneath her feet.

"Don't move," it said again.

Shortly, a van rumbled up and two men in masks and red hats got out. They grabbed her and roughly tossed her in the back.

As she rolled on her side while the men got back in the truck, she turned the phone's wireless on and texted Ramsey Dale.

"Dale help."

She put the phone away just as they got in and drove her into the compound.

***

Johnson walked into the kitchen of his mansion in Evergreen. His wife Ellen was doing the Wednesday Thanksgiving prep, having just ordered from Whole Foods. Turkey, fixings, half a case of fine Cabernet from one of their vineyards in Sonoma, a twelve-pack of Diet Pepsi for him, and her special spinach casserole. Not to mention the pumpkin pie and apple pie—Johnson's favorite, as it shouted America on an American holiday.

"When are the kids arriving?" he said.

"Jenny and Tom get here tonight around ten p.m." she responded. "Bobby is driving up tomorrow. Should be here in time for the end of the Macy's Parade. You know how they love to watch Santa Claus."

"Jesus, El, they're both in their twenties," Johnson sighed. "As long as it doesn't interfere with kickoff."

He walked out onto the deck, overlooking a forest of evergreen trees. Kickoff is what he was waiting for. McHenry and team would be expecting some sort of attack on the games, and security would be extra tight. Three pro games, in Detroit, Dallas, and Denver. And one college game in Oklahoma City, another city like Dallas, familiar with homegrown terrorism and national tragedy.

As the games progressed toward dinnertime, about the second half of the Cowboys/Niners game, the head fake would begin.

A bomb scare at Kennedy. An intercepted call about a hi-jacking coming in Toronto, just north of Detroit. A swarm of drone activity in New Hampshire, just above the Massachusetts border. The false alarms would start coming, but the head fake would be at the airports and ports, logical targets for an international terrorist group or a foreign-funded attack.

The terror alert would be activated, but people in the safety of their homes with their families would just be worried about getting back to where they came from on Sunday. Far as they were concerned, they were already in the safest place right now.

Until Friday morning.

The real attacks would start in the early Black Friday hours, East Coast time, with a truck bomb in the parking lot of the Westfield Garden State Plaza in New Jersey. From there, they would proceed to a high school football game in Evanston, Ill., outside Chicago. The Mall of America when it opens in early Midwest hours. A turkey trot outside of Nashville. A drone attack on the early college game in Columbia, Missouri. Then nothing for several hours as investigators and media tried to anticipate what was next.

Another head fake near the border in Waco as a bomb went off near the checkpoint, causing chaos and video reports of migrants streaming through the blown-out gates, as border police fired indiscriminately.

Then, a massive bomb in downtown Seattle, shattering windows for miles and taking out the Pike Place Fish Market at its busiest time in the early morning. Finally, and most dastardly, a column of tanks and military vehicles, with scores of militias dressed in U.S. Army fatigues and police uniforms driving down the strip of Las Vegas, firing with abandon at the morning revelers, arriving casino workers, and indeed, the casinos themselves.

As Nevada mobilized available forces, a firefight would erupt on the screens of horrified Americans, unable to process the sheer number of attacks.

Martial law would be inevitable. By the end of the day, Johnson thought with a smile, after a weekend of negotiations, Starks and his teams would be up and running by Monday, securing the country as he negotiated a new and unprecedented transfer of security power from McHenry and the U.S. government to a private enterprise—his own.

He had seen it done before, on a smaller level. Private militias and mercenary groups taking over the security of smaller countries. Blackwater founder Erik Prince once proposed taking overall security for U.S. troops in Afghanistan in exchange for access to its lucrative poppy crops. Wagner's Yevgeny Prigozhin in Africa.

But nobody had ever tried it at such a scale.

Starks had prepared teams of militia with headquarters in seven key areas of the country, reporting into Reno. No accountability to Denver. Mostly old airfields that had turned themselves into logistics centers for the nation's unregulated militias: Driggs, Idaho; Roanoke, Va.; Kenosha, Wis.; Lawrence, Mass.; etc.

Militiamen would be activated in waves over the weekend, with orders to secure key government offices, airports, train stations, and vital highway routes. No one group had any idea of the other. Each thought they were being called to defend and secure their area. By the time they were in place, a hierarchy would be activated reporting up to Starks, and by extension, Johnson.

If anything went wrong, almost everyone—except Starks and the regional leaders—would have some sort of plausible deniability.

It was perfect. A terrified nation, scared and angry at its government, would give up its freedom to a new force, one that would stand with them and guarantee the inequality and plundering of the elites would be over forever.

Johnson whistled as he went back into the kitchen to check the dressing.

Chapter 11

Ramsey knew what he had to do. The time for playing rogue cop was over. Hoken's wireless showed she had sent the text from Kenosha about fifteen minutes before her phone went dead. Time to bring in the big guns.

But he'd get a head start and was halfway to the Illinois/Wisconsin border in the Charger before he called his chief to request support. He knew they'd need to call Kenosha and Wisconsin state troopers too, as well as the FBI, as this was related to the drone strikes. He hoped it wasn't too late, and wasn't even sure what they'd find.

By the time he'd arrived in Kenosha, his bosses had radioed back that the FBI, nervous about the coming weekend, had notified Homeland Security, which said it would monitor. Resources were stretched across the country, and so it was agreed that local Kenosha police would pay a routine visit to the airfield to sniff around.

Kenosha police had been gun-shy, so to speak, for the last several years after one of their own shot an unarmed black man, reigniting nationwide protests and riots. They no doubt knew that local militias marched in and around the airfield, including many of the troublemakers who had taken on the protesters and looters and generally made a bad situation worse.

Ramsey tuned into the local Kenosha police scanner in time to hear the squad car had been stopped at the gate, and then let in and over to one of the larger hangers. Fifteen minutes later, as Ramsey himself approached the turn-off to the trunk road leading to the airfield, the scanner carried one of the officer's voices, saying they'd found nothing. Just business as usual. Ramsey was heading down the trunk road as the squad car passed him at high speed, heading in the other direction. He waved his hand out the window to stop them, but they rushed past him at about 70 mph. Ramsey turned back toward the airfield. He was suspicious.

Whatever was happening, if there was something going on there, the people inside had now been alerted. As he drove past the front gate, Ramsey watched as armored vehicles rolled up, followed by a half dozen gun-toting militiamen. A bit intense for the day before Thanksgiving.

He needed to get inside, but obviously pulling up and announcing himself wouldn't work. He drove around back. As he did, he felt it before he could see it. Looking to his right out the passenger side, an armed drone was pacing him. No faster, no slower. Not pointing. Just there. He'd been spotted but not stopped. Ramsey turned left at a junction and headed away from the airfield. After about half a mile, the drone disappeared. He needed a different way in.

Ramsey saw a couple of delivery trucks making their way out of the East gate and headed toward Highway 41. He followed them about seven miles outside of town to an old farm. It looked like a battlefield. Obviously used for shooting practice and perhaps as a stopping point for sensitive deliveries and or escapes. Once the drivers were inside, he parked a half mile down the road and hiked back. The place was just about empty, and the grey barn door swung open in the early evening wind. Ramsey walked calmly toward it, looking over his shoulder but seeing nothing from the house. When he got to the door, he drew a breath. It was the squad car.

Ramsey looked in and saw the keys in the front seat. Nobody around. Time for fun and games was over. He hopped in, took a deep breath, and turned the ignition. He gunned the car out of the barn, slamming the door in the process and racing across the field for the road. A few seconds later, a bullet slammed into the back windshield, then another crashed against his side mirror. Whoever was there was not happy. Time was growing short now. He shot past his Charger and back toward town. He ignored the police radio and called his boss from his phone.

Just as he answered, he looked in his rear-view mirror and saw the truck gaining.

***

Hoken looked on in growing horror as the action picked up in the control tower. Rather than the dusty old airfield monitoring system she had expected, the tower had been refitted with the latest computers, radar systems, and wireless systems. It looked like a cross between NASA and an Amazon fulfillment center she had once seen in South Chicago.

On the screens were videos of vast rows of weaponry and hardware, from tanks to jeeps to drones. Hundreds of drones. They were lined up inside the hangar, and the hanger behind it, and the one behind that. A giant X-shaped desk sat in the middle of the room and in the slot was an engineer barking orders.

In the corner, Miller stood conversing with another engineer. He had not paid attention to her since she had been taken up to the control room from her holding cell twenty minutes ago. She had left behind the two police officers, beaten senseless but alive. Now Miller was walking toward her.

"If you had wanted an interview, you simply could have called, Miss... Hoken."

She said nothing.

"I don't like trespassers, especially when I'm busy."

"It looks like you're about to start a war," Hoken said.

"Perhaps, but also maybe stop one," he said as he looked into her eyes from above. "The people in this state... in this country are tired of being afraid in their own homes, in their own communities. The security services, police, or whatever you want to call them, are corrupt, ill-trained, uneducated, and wholly lacking in the ability to keep law and order. They've been pulled every which way by left and right forces, to the point where they simply stopped doing their jobs for fear of losing their jobs. We are going to fix that."

"How... By killing people with these things?" She wished she had her tape recorder to turn on or her phone recorder.

"Technology has come a long way, Miss Hoken. And law enforcement, at least in this country, hasn't kept up. Our brethren in China, Russia, Israel, even the UK, are much more advanced in how they track and record civil movements, and therefore they have less crime. Less abuse. More civil societies."

"Two of those countries are authoritarian, and the other two are playing defense against homegrown terrorism," she said.

"We have that here too. You remember Oklahoma City, Vegas. Even Portland," he said.

"And thanks to you, or your friends, Chicago, San Francisco, Boston, and who knows what next," she shot back.

"You will know shortly, Miss Hoken," Miller said. "And so will everybody else. In the meantime, I've arranged for you to see a long-lost friend."

He turned around just as Sadowski entered the room. Hoken's blue eyes widened and she squirmed unconsciously, but said nothing.

"We meet again. Perhaps now we can finish off before we were so rudely interrupted," Sadowski said. He bent down and whispered something in her ear which made her swing her two tied hands toward his head. Sadowski grabbed her hands and held them near his pants. "Later," he whispered.

Miller had returned to the X-shaped console. Hoken heard someone say 'Reno' and handed a phone line to him. He mumbled a few things, then barked at the slot man. "Flight patterns coordinated with central time schemes?"

"Yes, sir," the slot man said. "Friday 11:07."

Miller nodded and turned back to the phone, said something, and hung up.

"I'm afraid my Thanksgiving table is full," Miss Hoken. "But I'm sure Mr. Sadowski here can find an alternative way for you to… celebrate."

He walked out of the room. Sadowski grabbed Hoken and brought her back to her holding room with the cops. "See you soon," he promised, smacking her ass as he pushed her in.

Hoken strained to put the pieces together. What does someone in Reno have to do with an attack on Chicago, or Kenosha for that matter? She needed to get out, not for the least of reasons to avoid another run-in with Sadowski. One of the cops had come to and was groaning. She asked him if he knew where he was. And did he have any communication device?

He felt for his radio, his gun, his club, his phone. All removed. Then he grabbed his wrist. He still had his Apple Watch. "This might work," he said. "As long as whoever has my phone isn't monitoring it."

"I'm Lindsey. What's your name?"

"Chris."

"Chris, something terrible is going to happen. We have to get out of here tonight," she said, rubbing his bleeding head with his jacket.

He sat up, played with his watch, and dialed a number.

"This is Officer Chris Jackson," he said, reaching central Kenosha dispatch. "Officer Murphy and I are down, our car is gone, and we're trapped in some building with a female citizen."

"We can monitor your signal," the dispatch said. "Your car reported all clear several hours ago but since then we haven't been able to reach it."

Dispatch opened up the line. "All units, we have contact with Jackson and Murphy but their car is missing. Be on the lookout for unit 56. It is likely stolen.

"Request all available units report to Dawn Field. Possible hostage situation."

Ramsey heard the radio and looked back again. The truck was within shooting distance now. He needed to get to a highway where he would attract more attention. He swerved to the right and through a fence, across a small baseball diamond. Several shots came from the passenger window of the truck behind as it chased him across the empty field. Ramsey ducked low and headed straight for left field. He crashed through the Spotted Cow sign next to the foul pole and made a line through the parking lot toward the highway. If he could get out of the parking lot, he might be okay.

Four more shots fired as the truck blasted through the fence in pursuit. But by this time, Ramsey had opened up a distance and spun around the back of a miniature golf course. As he sped up the highway ramp, the truck began gaining again. But once on the highway, he had other problems. Another squad car had spotted him and was in pursuit, its red light and siren flashing.

The truck faded back and disappeared. Ramsey got on the radio. "This is unit 56 on 41 heading South toward

Dawn Field. My name is Lt. Dale Ramsey from Chicago PD. I did NOT steal this car. I stole it BACK. One of your units is tailing me, but we have to get back to Dawn Field. Can anyone hear me?"

"Lt. Ramsey, pull over ASAP," the voice on the radio said. "Our officers will assist you once you have safely stopped."

"No can do, ma'am," Ramsey said. "I've got someone hostage inside that air base just as you do. Should be there in five minutes. I suspect they are heavily armed. Can you call in Wisconsin Highway Patrol, and the FBI?"

"Not until you stop safely and identify yourself, sir."

The trailing squad car pulled behind Ramsey and tried to get him to stop through its external speaker, but he kept going. Both cars pulled off the highway and on to the trunk road heading toward the airfield. As they approached, Ramsey saw three more squad cars blocking his way to the gate. The jig was up, and he prepared to stop. Maybe he could convince them before he was cuffed.

Just then he saw the drones come over the fence.

***

Starks took the call from Peter Miller. He had ordered radio silence in the thirty-six hours before the operation, but Miller texted it was an emergency.

"What's going on," Starks barked.

"We have an issue. Some reporter and a couple of cops have showed up, and we had to take them in. Now we got more cops at the door."

"You need to get the team out of their before they shut you down. We're too close."

"I will. No worries. We'll be ready for New Trier," Miller said.

He hung up and barked orders to the X-shaped desk.

"Establish a perimeter, no shooting. We need a diversion," he said.

Stalking to the other side, he said, "Send out Squads A-F, low, below the tree line toward the lake, then out over the water at no more than ten feet, to our alternative site."

Turning back to the first engineer, he said, "Deploy smoke screen."

As Ramsey sat in his car, awaiting a swarm of cops about to surround him, he saw the drones dip and pass over, spreading purple smoke. What was it? Some sort of poisonous gas? It stopped the troopers in their tracks, and one of them reached for his radio.

"We're getting smoked out. Request backup," the radio squawked in Ramsey's car. Suddenly he knew what it was. A diversion. Something was happening. During the mayhem, he gunned the cruiser, blasting through the squad cars, and headed straight for the gate. He caught the drones by surprise and was crashing through before the engineers could raise the alarm and Miller could give the fire order. By the time he did, Ramsey was in. The other cops weren't so lucky. The drones leveled on them through the smoke and cut them down in a hail of bullets. Against orders, Miller had started a small war.

Ramsey was inside before Miller knew it, heading toward the control room. For all the drone protection, the control tower was surprisingly unguarded. One guard came running at him, but Ramsey slammed him with the butt of his Beretta. As he turned back toward the control room, Sadowski stepped in front, his gun leveled.

"About time I got to thank you for fucking up my bar," he growled.

Ramsey needed three seconds. "Where is the girl?" he shouted.

"You don't need to worry about her. We're going to finish what you interrupted. But that's none of your business."

Sadowski smiled, but Ramsey used the time he took to imagine what he would do to Hoken to leap back three feet and race down a hallway. By the time Sadowski turned the corner to fire, Ramsey was through another door, headed toward the hangar.

He banged through another room and stopped to shove a desk against the door. He got out just as Sadowski started firing through the door, pushing against the desk with his immense weight. Ramsey crashed through another door and into the hangar, just in time to witness an extraordinary spectacle: two hundred fifty drones, rising like a buzzing hive of bees to ten feet above the ground, and then filing out the hangar in order, five at a time.

Ramsey gaped at the drones, then turned and grabbed a stray drone shell, made of magnesium alloy, which was light but strong. As Sadowski came rushing through the door, Ramsey swung it with all his might at his face. He collapsed in a heap, still holding the gun. Ramsey kicked his hand and kneeled down, punched him twice in the face, knocking him out. He grabbed the gun and ran to the far side of the hangar—another door.

"Lindsey!" he shouted.

"In here!" she screamed back. She had heard the buzzing of the drones and was terrified. He kicked open the door and saw Hoken standing there, the two cops just behind her.

"Lieutenant Ramsey, Chicago Police Force," he shouted. "Let's get out of here. Reinforcements are coming."

Ramsey led them out the hangar door, which was wide open. Immediately, they were fired on by a dozen drones speeding around the perimeter. They leaped back inside, and one of the cops shut the door.

"We're under attack out front too. Hopefully, your brethren can send help."

"What can we do?" said Hoken.

Ramsey motioned them to follow. As they came upon the first guard, he kneeled down and grabbed his gun. He gave it to one of the cops.

Ramsey and the cops burst into the control room, with Hoken not far behind. Miller turned, surprised. He nodded to a guard nearby who drew his gun, but the cop shot him point-blank.

Miller reached to the control board and barked something into a microphone. "Commence escape strategy," he said, flicking off the switch and slowly raising his hands.

Soon, every drone around the perimeter was gone, leaving just the group in the control room and a gathering force of police outside.

"Everybody back away from the controls," Ramsey barked. Miller and a half dozen engineers stood and backed away.

"You're too late," said Miller.

Ramsey and Hoken went to the control panel while the other cop grabbed the guard's gun, and together they held the engineers as more police entered the airfield.

"I don't see any way to get them back," Hoken said.

"They're not coming back," Miller laughed. "In a war, retreat protocols are normal. They will regroup, under alternate orders."

Ramsey and Hoken looked at each other. "What were their original orders?"

Miller shrugged.

"What war are you talking about?" said Hoken.

"The one you are already fighting," he laughed again. Police began streaming into the control room and secured the rest of the airfield. Hoken borrowed Ramsey's phone while she searched for hers, and called her newsroom. This would be one helluva Thanksgiving Eve story.

***

Starks swore as the news came in that Miller and his team had been de-activated. He had expected something like this would happen, but with each passing hour had gotten more confident. Chicago again. Those fuckups. Now they'd have to go to alternate planning. No big deal. The drones had been evacuated and were in a holding pattern, still available to carry out their mission. The question was what this would do to the investigation to track them down.

Police had access to the control room, though if Miller and his engineers had followed protocol, they would have deleted all relevant files. He had no choice but to continue. He dreaded calling Johnson but knew he had to. He'd want to know what happened once he realized the logistics had changed, and Starks had been around military operations too long to know that "no surprises" meant no surprises. He punched in the number.

If anything, the Kenosha raid could simply play into the false narrative they hoped to set for Thanksgiving Day.

***

"New terror attack halted in Kenosha, Wis.," screamed the headlines that evening. The story played out across the country as the lead item the night before Thanksgiving, and security was being tightened everywhere from the Macy's Thanksgiving Day parade in New York to jammed airports around the country.

President McHenry, at Camp David for the holiday, convened an emergency cabinet meeting over a secured video monitor to discuss the ramifications. The FBI had taken over the Kenosha investigation from its field office in Chicago; its cybercrime experts poring over what was available in Miller's systems at the airfield.

"Was this attack for tomorrow?" McHenry asked Homeland Security Secretary Pastor.

"We don't know," Mr. President. "Our team is working with FBI cybercrime to break into their systems now. We're not even sure there was even an attack planned. But we do know that this is where the killer drones lived and that they escaped during the operation."

"Escaped? Escaped? How do drones escape? Doesn't somebody control them? Didn't we seize the control room? Shouldn't they just be lying on the ground inoperative right now?"

"They might be," Pastor said. "But wherever they were going, they got their first. Right now, we're operating under the preventative assumption that they are still active and could be activated by... someone," Pastor said.

"Chicago. Boston. San Francisco. These Kenosha drones couldn't have possibly been involved in all three," McHenry said.

"We don't know that, but I think it's a safe assumption, Mr. President."

"If it's true, then there could be other – operating centers for lack of a better word. And they could be anywhere."

"What do we have on Peter Miller? He's a political player, I know. But anything that connects him to any of those three cities. Or what about Johnson?"

"Johnson and Miller go back, in political fundraising circles. Miller had invested a few million in Johnson's asset management business. But nothing so far that ties them together in any extreme political movement, or terrorist thing."

"He's big in the logistics business. Flying farm equipment around the country for big corporations. There are some reports he helps support local militias in Wisconsin by shipping in weapons. The airfield has been used before as a landing strip for re-routing equipment used by the military consultants.

"So, he has a military record?" McHenry said.

"Yes, Mr. President," said Defense Secretary Tim Hayes, "...Marines. Iraq. Fallujah it seems. Served his time and was honorably discharged in 2012."

"Any connections with ISIS?" McHenry said.

"That was just before ISIS burst onto the scene, but it's probable our boys on the ground had a better idea what was happening than the rest of the world," Hayes said.

Pastor added "Just to be certain, we're running traces on everybody in his unit," to see if there are any suspicious connections."

"Do you want us to do that?" Hayes said.

"We got it," Pastor said. "Also, Nikki, I think Homeland Security should take over Kenosha. It's our remit after all."

Forrester shot a look at him. "It's everyone's remit."

McHenry shut them both up. "This is no fucking time to be territorial. Work together, Goddammit! We've got to find those Goddam drones. Today!" he shouted.

"We're lucky the country is in veritable lockdown tomorrow," Pastor said. "But we've increased security in all ports, airports, and train stations, and we'll be monitoring the Macy's parade, the big football games, and anywhere else homegrown terrorists might make a splash.

"Okay, I want an update every three hours on the cyber systems. And another meeting at this time tomorrow. Sorry folks. Now I've got to brief Ginny. This is going to be her mess in two months."

***

Hoken monitored the headlines on two of her screens. CNN on TV and social media on her iPad. Typical speculation about the drones. No comments from authorities. Stretchy stories trying to tie the incident to the ruckus in Kenosha with that kid years ago. A few news groups had a little about Peter Miller, but nothing more than that he had gotten into trouble rigging horse races years ago. One said he had a military background.

She fidgeted on her couch. She'd called her parents and told them she wasn't coming back for Thanksgiving after all because she had to work the Kenosha story. She left out her role in it, for now. Her first-person reports would hit the airwaves tomorrow. Then the calls would come in from national media looking for a story tied to the attacks to fill the air on a slow news day. She could wait.

She eyed her phone. Then grabbed it and dialed Ramsey.

"There's something horribly unattended here," she blurted as he answered the phone.

"Hello to you too, Lindsey."

"This can't be the end of it. It's too easy. The drones are still missing. Everybody is treating this like we've solved the case. The drones are still missing."

"I know. My contact at the FBI field office here assures me the authorities don't see it that way. They are worried about the drones. But they're more worried there are other airfields. You don't launch national terrorist attacks from Kenosha."

"Yeah, that makes sense. So, Miller isn't the mastermind."

"Guy couldn't even rig horse races much less mastermind a national terrorist plot," said Ramsey. "He was obviously working with someone, and I'm not yet sure where the FBI is going with this. But they have their leads. I'll keep you informed."

"What am I supposed to do, just sit here?"

"If you want you can come over," Ramsey said.

Hoken looked at her phone. "Very forward of you Detective Ramsey. And in the middle of a case, no less."

Ramsey laughed. "I have grown quite fond of you, Miss Hoken. But what I mean is that if you want, you can help me go through a computer file. You see, in the ensuing hubbub around the arrest of Miller and his team, I stuck a USB file into one of their computers, which was still on. He deactivated the central control panel before we got to him. But this computer was on the side of the room. Might have even been his personal one. Or not. But there is some info on it I think you might want to see."

Hoken took a deep breath. There had to be more to this story. Maybe it was on that file. She'd take her chance and go.

"I'll come by in the morning," she said.

"I'll make the turkey sandwiches," he replied.

Chapter 12

Thanksgiving Day dawned bright and chilly in Chicago and was generally clear on the East Coast as well. There was still a heatwave out West, but clear for the high school football games.

In New York City, the Macy's Thanksgiving Day Parade went off without a hitch. Government forces monitored the skies, the seas, even the sewers for possible terrorist activity, but by the time Santa Claus appeared and people started to leave, all was quiet.

Security was tighter at Ford Field in Detroit for the first football game between the Lions and the Green Bay Packers, including fly-over drones and airspace monitoring by the Selfridge Air National Guard Base nearby.

McHenry watched closely from Camp David, his secure phone at his side. The morning cabinet meeting went off without a hitch, but still no sign of the drones.

In Reno, Starks had the game on over on the side of his large study, a hunting lodge motif with several big game trophies hanging on the walls. In front of him sat a bank of computers with encrypted connections to the regional command centers. He pinged Lawrence.

"Cluster Lambda, command center checking in. Ready for deployment in T-minus three?"

"Lambda here, ready. Skies are clear."

"Out," Starks said. He picked up the phone and called Johnson. "All set for the end of halftime," he added, referring to the Cowboys-Niners game starting in a few hours.

Johnson nodded his head and hung up. He had written his message to President McHenry all ready, offering his services at precisely the right time on Friday.

In Chicago, Hoken rang the bell at Ramsey's Southside apartment, a three-story walk-up where you could just see Millennium Park and the lake to the North if you stretched your neck out over the rickety, wooden back balcony. He opened the door and let her in, still wearing his gun.

"Ah, early White Sox. Very chic," she joked as she entered his living room. It was surprisingly clean and could have passed for modern, if not for all the White Sox paraphernalia on the walls. The television was turned to CNN, which was broadcasting another story about tighter security that day.

"Happy Thanksgiving," he said. "Sandwiches are in the fridge. Soda or water. Or if you want a beer, I have that too. The Niners-Cowboys game starts in an hour."

"Maybe then," she said. "Let's see what you got."

Ramsey sat down at a cluttered table with his laptop at the center. He pulled up a chair beside him and motioned Hoken to sit.

"I'm pretty sure this is a private drive Miller kept, maybe to ensure some measure of self-preservation. It's got a ton of files about horses and jockeys, tracks around the Midwest, bloodlines, etc. There are a few business files, but they seem mostly tied to the logistics. For example, this one is titled Fargo. It seems to be details of a contract with a tractor manufacturer to transport heavy equipment from North Dakota to Kenosha and then to truck it around Wisconsin and upper Illinois. This one is called Quad. It's a similar contract with an irrigation equipment company in the Quad Cities in Iowa. We also have Duluth, Battle Creek, Omaha, Dayton, and Reno. For a guy who likes to name horses, he doesn't have much imagination when it comes to computer files."

Hoken simply nodded and looked at his face, ten inches away from hers. Seems he had shaved his stubble earlier in the day. She turned back to the screen.

"Then there's this one. Panther."

"Is it a horse?" Hoken said.

"No. The Black Panther Militia Group is one of eight known militias operating illegally in Wisconsin, and more than twenty-five that we don't even know have names. It's a list of phone numbers, with codenames tied to them. I've sent them over to the FBI already to see if they turn anything up."

"Do you think these militias could have something to do with the attacks?" Hoken said. "I thought their mission was to protect their territories from intruders, government, and others. Why would they attack in another state?"

"I don't know," Ramsey said, sitting back and looking at her. "Maybe the numbers will turn something up."

Hoken looked at him again for a lingering minute, then turned back to the screen.

"What is Reno? That's not a farming town, is it?"

"More of a ranching area, but yes, there are some farms. Let's see. I don't think I looked at that one," he said, calling it up.

"What have we here," he said. The file contained more numbers and code names. It wasn't an equipment-hauling contract like the others. But the names seemed more military to Ramsey. Op Charlie, regional comm, Bonanza, Light Horse, Starfucker.

"Who is Starfucker?" Hoken said. Just a number and a text. Ramsey tried the number. No answer, no message. Just right to voicemail. Ramsey hung up. He looked again at the names. Light Horse seemed familiar. Then it hit him.

"This is interesting," he said. Hoken looked up.

"Light Horse was the name given to Australian militias back in the early 1900s. Several of them were brought together to fight in World War I and were spectacularly crushed in the Gallipoli campaign in Turkey," Ramsey said, remembering his books on World War I. "Whoever is behind this is a military buff of major proportions."

"How do you know that stuff?" Hoken asked.

"I always liked history. Read 'The Art of War' and a lot of Churchill's stuff from the world wars," he answered, as he began to look up Gallipoli on his phone.

"Hmm," murmured Hoken, thinking absently that there might be more to this guy than the White Sox. Suddenly she was startled.

"Look at this. Down at the bottom." Ramsey peered in close, their heads side by side.

"Squad signals Kappa go, Kappa hold, Kappa engage, Kappa retreat. What is Kappa?" she said.

"I don't know, but they appear to be signals to a force. Maybe a militia. Maybe a drone team," Ramsey said. "And look at these numbers underneath each one. They look like codes of some sort. 674#K921. Could this be how his team controlled the drones? Through a preset program activated by these commands?

"I don't know, but I'll send this right away to the boys. They'll have a better understanding."

He pushed the forward button and pounded out a few orders. A few seconds later, a reply confirmed the file had been received. Then Bledsoe appeared in a video chat room.

"Lt. Ramsey, hello, and happy Thanksgiving."

"You get the short straw, agent, uh…"

"Bledsoe sir. Yes, so to speak. I'll be off tonight and get some family time. But we're all hands right now with all these threats. We'll take a look at these codes right away. Where did you get them?"

"Left behind in the Wisconsin raid," Ramsey said, not wanting to give up anymore. "What do you make of them?"

"We'll run them through our encryption programs, but off the top of my head, I'd say they are a short list of computerized commands. Using something like this, someone could control a digital device with just his—or her—phone. Providing they've been pre-programmed."

"They look like military commands or nicknames," Ramsey said.

"Maybe, but not the type we would see if any of our militaries launched an attack," said Bledsoe. "They are more like field commands. The types of things you'd hear from a squadron leader in the field, then a general at headquarters. Whoever these belong to is accustomed to barking orders. Might be a lead for us. We'll run these through our programs and get back to you with any details. Happy Thanksgiving, sir."

"Thanks, agent, uh…"

"Bledsoe sir."

Ramsey hung up and turned his head toward Hoken. "Nothing to do now but wait. How about that beer?"

She smiled and brushed her hair back. "Maybe later," she said, looking up at him. He leaned in and kissed her lightly, looking at her closed eyes as she welcomed him, and delicately flicking her lips with his tongue.

She opened up, and embracing together, they stood up and pressed close. She reached for his shirt and began unbuttoning while he pulled at her blouse, rubbing his hands on her bare back and pulling it up at the same time until it was over her head. Hoken and had no bra on and both shirtless, they fell back on his bed, engulfed by the tingling anticipation that happens when two naked bodies come together.

The only sound was the football game on in the living room.

**

The USA Today news alert flashed first across phones, then CNN broadcast it in a strip across video screens as the Cowboys kicked off for the second half.

"Bomb Scare at Kennedy Airport in New York."

McHenry picked up his phone to Homeland Security.

"It's a bag in the international terminal," said Pastor. "We're evacuating now."

"Any drone activity," McHenry said.

"Negative."

Most folks went back to the game. Those who switched to the cable networks were greeted with the usual videos of people standing around outside. The news trucks rushed to the airport.

An hour later, the second one came. Possible hijacking in Toronto.

This time the networks cut into the game, noting the "trend" of two airport scares in less than an hour. Still nothing concrete.

Then, as the Cowboys were driving in the final two minutes of the game, the drones.

"Mr. President, we've picked up a swarm of drones on radar on the Canadian border just above New Hampshire," Pastor called in.

"Where are they headed?" McHenry said.

"Nowhere definitive yet. They seem to be assembling."

"Can we get air cover up there?

"On its way, sir."

NBC News broke into the post-game analysis with the latest update, noting that Homeland Security had picked up something to do with drones in the Northeast.

Hoken and Ramsey watched from his bed. She had pulled on one of his old Bears jerseys and was sitting at the foot of the bed. Ramsey lay back on two pillows and smoked a cigarette, just like in the movies.

"Lots of activity," she said. "Something doesn't seem right."

"You're right. The last three attacks have been surprises, not broadcast like this. Also, the fact that we can pick the drones up on the radar this time seems odd."

Finally, as the third game was about to start, a terrorist attack warning phoned into the Port of Oakland, one of the largest shipping points on the West Coast.

Pastor activated the terror alert warning to orange, for high risk. The news alerts flashed across screens and phones worldwide.

"Sir, we've gotten to the drones. They are hovering, assembling, at about 5,000 feet, just over the border. We're in touch with Canadian intelligence, and they are trying to ascertain where they came from."

"Get me Prime Minister Clatchey," McHenry said to an aide. "What about Toronto?"

"False alarm, it seems," said Pastor. "We're monitoring, but planes are taking off without incident. "We've asked that they delay in-coming flights for two hours, and they've complied."

"Can we shoot those drones down?" McHenry said.

"We could, but right now it's more useful for our team to study their communication wavelengths. Try to figure out how they're operating. Our investigators are receiving many tips with possible coding patterns, and we're going through those now."

***

Ramsey pulled some jeans on and got out of bed, went to the fridge, and cracked a beer. He handed it to Hoken, who took a sip and handed it back.

"I don't like this. Too easy. Too expected," he said. "Feels almost like, like a decoy."

She brushed back her hair and looked hard at the computer screen. She picked up her phone and dialed the Reno number again.

Someone answered.

"Report," a male voice barked.

"Looking for Starfucker," Hoken said, in her most official voice.

Silence, then disconnect.

She looked at Ramsey. "Can you trace the number?"

"Give me twenty minutes," he said, picking up his phone and putting his hand on her shoulder.

Starks threw the phone away in disgust. A classic rookie mistake. He'd been so excited by the impact of the decoys he had forgotten the Chicago group had been compromised. He reached into his drawer and grabbed another burner. He called Bangor.

"Report," he shouted.

"All well. Bit of a standoff up above Jay Peak," came the reply. "The drones had moved over toward northern Vermont, tracked by the air force."

"Okay. Back to you in the new dawn," Starks said.

Despite the snafus, things were going well. The Feds were running around, doing what they do, and the plan was moving forward. He checked his coordinates one more time, and then the timeline, and sat down to watch the final game.

Chapter 13

Marcia Harris was standing in line outside Target at the Westfield Garden State Mall Friday morning, reading her Apple news feed for clues about the New Hampshire drones when the bomb went off.

Her children had warned her at the Thanksgiving table the day before about going to public places with all these alerts going off around the country, but Marcia was a Black Friday traditionalist, and she never missed a sale. In past years, she and some friends would don war paint, mix a thermos of Bloody Marys, and lay siege to the malls before dawn. It was all part of the holiday fun.

In recent years, as digital shopping largely replaced mall shopping, the attraction of Black Friday had begun to wear off, with retailers making their sales available even before Thanksgiving. Marcia didn't care. As far as she was concerned, it made the lines shorter.

She was standing only a quarter mile away from the truck bomb at the other end of the mall outside the Macy's, but the sound of the explosion and the flashing light shocked her, and she dropped her phone.

Chaos erupted as crowds ran in every direction. Mall security and police struggled to get to the blast zone, leaping over bloody bodies and pushing against people racing to find their families. Harris yelped and stood motionless as the smoke covered the blast zone, wondering whether to run or pick up her phone and take a photo. Police were moving in, so she stayed where she was.

Two minutes later, as a confused crowd began moving in a more orderly fashion away from the blast toward Target, a second bomb detonated in a car just 100 yards away. It was the age-old terrorist tactic of setting off one explosion to move a crowd in a certain direction, and then set off a bigger one where they gathered.

Harris was thrown to the ground and the windows behind her shattered. The man next to her had nails sticking out of his head and torso, and was thrashing wildly on the pavement. Harris touched her face and saw blood all over her hand. She screamed.

Fifteen yards away, someone raised a pistol and fired into the air. Everybody move this way," the razor-haired, blonde man shouted. He began aiming his gun at people moving in the other direction. "This way."

As police moved in, the man shouted "I got this."

"Drop the gun," one officer shouted.

"Do your job," the man countered, and started pointing the pistol at him. The cop shot him in the chest.

Rather than calm things, the shooting ignited the crowd, turning their fear and confusion into a brittle anger and causing several young men to lunge at the officer, kicking his gun away and pushing him to the ground. As fellow officers descended on the scene, a brawl ensued, ending when another officer fired into the air and addressed the crowd with a bullhorn.

"Everybody freeze and stay down. We don't know if this is over yet."

Overhead, two drones buzzed quietly as they streamed the scene. News trucks rumbled into the parking lot just as the crowd started to notice the drones.

"There they are," shouted one woman, pulling a pistol from her purse and firing in their direction."

Another man grabbed the gun from her as several more folks brandished firearms and pointed them toward the drones.

Harris crawled across the parking lot and propped herself up against the wall of Target, wondering where her purse and phone had gone. A jagged scar ran down her right cheek, and her hands were covered in blood. A shooting pain ran down her left leg.

As she watched the scene unfold, she couldn't make out who was in control. The police and armed crowd were pointing guns at each other. Everyone was shooting at the drones. Three cars down the parking lot, she saw two men, pistols in the air, charging toward her with a shopping cart.

She curled into a ball and turned her head away, but they ran right by and into the Target.

Curtis Lanier and his brother hadn't come to the mall that day to loot. They were there to rob Black Friday shoppers in the parking lot. Maybe steal a car. As they sat in his brother's twelve-year-old, dirty white Dodge Ram, taking a bump of cocaine before a busy day outside, the first explosion rocked the car from under them. The second blew the windshield.

The men staggered out of the truck covered in glass and bleeding superficially. Curtis coughed, then touched his Taurus G3 pistol in his waist, and put his hand on his brother's back.

"Come on, man. This is our chance." The two men grabbed a shopping cart and charged toward the Target, where people were milling around at the entrance, unsure whether to retreat inside or make a run for it into the chaos.

Curtis and his brother raced for an open side door, past a disheveled Harris, and inside toward the electronics aisle. They were soon joined by scores of others, who had sufficiently recovered from the shock to realize this Black Friday everything might be free of charge.

Fighting broke out in the store. The manager told all staff on the loudspeaker to run. Harris watched from her perch as more police arrived, and a few charged into the store to confront the looters, Thanksgiving shoppers, and anyone else unlucky enough to be in their way.

One cop came around a corner and put his hand on Curtis' shopping cart, by this time already full of TV and computer boxes. Curtis tugged back, and his brother swung at the officer, knocking him into a shelf of printers. His partner pointed his gun at the young men. Curtis pulled out his Taurus, but before he could aim, a shot hit him in the right shoulder, causing him to drop his gun and spin to the ground.

As the two cops leaped on him, his brother grabbed the cart and fled through the crowds and smoke. Harris watched him sprinting through the parking lot with his cart. For just a brief moment, she wondered if he had grabbed the last printer. Then she passed out.

In the WBBM newsroom in Chicago, Joan Grantwell was monitoring the CNN footage from New Jersey when a call came in from one of the sports stringers.

"There's been a drone attack at the New Trier High School football game in Evanston," a sports desk editor shouted from across the newsroom. "People are down, and the crowd is scattering. Still no police on the scene."

"Tell the reporter to find a safe spot but stay on the scene," Grantwell barked. The squawk box at the city desk suddenly sprang to life, with police calling in from several points at once.

Grantwell looked around the newsroom. Holiday skeleton staff. Mostly sports reporters for the games and a handful of business reporters covering Black Friday. She thought of Hoken but couldn't find her. She reached for her phone but was distracted by another report of an explosion at a Turkey Trot in Nashville, in what was being described as a land mine.

She put down the phone and barked to the assistant city editor.

"Let's get all hands in. It's game on!"

***

Ramsey and Hoken had landed in Reno and were just getting into a rental car, heading forty-five minutes north toward Lake Tahoe, when they heard the radio reports from New Jersey. Minutes later, they heard about Evanston.

Hoken thought to call her newsroom. She knew they would be pissed at her for being away, but she had taken the time anyway and was supposed to be in Wisconsin. As she expected, pandemonium. She told Grantwell she was in fact in Nevada and was pursuing a lead. Grantwell was not impressed. Told her to get back as soon as possible.

Hoken hung up and looked ahead. "How much farther?"

"Just up the hills a bit. Maybe thirty-five minutes to North Lake," Ramsey said.

His men had tracked the phone signal to a neighborhood just outside of Incline Village before the signal died. Neither the detective nor the reporter had any idea how they would pinpoint it, but it occurred to Ramsey that they might have better luck viewing the neighborhood from the water. So, they headed to a public boathouse.

The boathouse was closed for the winter and was in the process of changing over to a ski rental and snowmobile shop. But the manager had been listening to the reports of the terror attacks over the radio, and he reacted to Ramsey's badge.

"You can borrow my speedboat," the manager said. "But tell me, are you worried about an attack here?"

As he said that, he pulled a shotgun off a shelf underneath the cash register. Ramsey and Hoken nodded at him.

"Always good to be safe, but we're just on a bit of a fishing expedition. Have you heard of anyone around here goes by the name of Starfucker?"

"No," said the manager. "Lots of eccentrics here though. Military types too."

"Really?" Hoken said.

"They like the freedom of the mountains. They can hide and move around at ease."

"I don't know if I can help, but I've seen a star marking on a boat about a mile down the coast," said a young man who was changing the signs in the back, and had been overhearing.

Graham Hughes was home from college at Cal and had been for the last few weeks since the drone attack had killed his girlfriend, Darla. He'd been working in the store and planned to save enough money through the holiday season to quit school and join the police. He was determined to make someone pay for what had happened.

"What do you mean, a star," Ramsey said.

"Just a gold star, like the type they put on your chest in the army," Hughes said. "On the back of some guy's boat. Just saying."

"Well, let's start there. You know these waters?"

"Lived here my whole life," the kid said.

"Okay, come on."

Ramsey and Hughes and Hoken loaded into the boat and took off slowly, puttering down the coast and looking at the lakeside mansions outside Incline Village. A stiff wind worked the current against them. Hoken sat in the back, scanning news feeds on her phone, while Hughes pointed the way to Ramsey. As they rounded a tree-lined bend, the house and dock suddenly appeared, pushed back into the trees. If they had been a quarter mile further out in the lake, they might have missed it completely.

Ramsey cut the engine and they coasted closer to the dock. Using binoculars Ramsey found on the control center, he peered forward and saw the gold star on the back of the boat. There was no name. Just the star.

"Starfucker," he said to himself.

"You know the address of this house?" Ramsey asked Hughes.

"No, these are private roads. Very difficult to even get on them. I'm sure there is a name but I don't know it."

Ramsey snapped a few photos and forwarded them back to the team in Chicago.

"Get me closer. I want to see what's on board."

There was no sign of activity in the house, so as they approached, Ramsey grabbed the side of the vessel and leaped over the rail.

Hoken took a few more photos while Hughes idled the engine.

Ramsey crouched down and went toward the cabin. Locked. He climbed up to the steering wheel and opened the control panel. A gun. Loaded. And keys. Everything was set up for a quick getaway. Out of curiosity he grabbed the radio and turned it on, glancing at the frequency. It was turned to twenty-five, not a standard boating frequency.

Ramsey was about to speak into it when he heard the shot.

***

Hoken screamed as Hughes was blown off the helm, a bloody hole in his shoulder. He fell back 10 feet and landed with a thud next to her, grasping his arm in agony. The boat began to drift away.

Ramsey ran to the bow and leaped across into the well of their boat just in time, crashing close to Hughes and grabbing a cushion, and pushing it on his shoulder. He looked up and saw Hoken trying to grab the wheel. Then back at the house. Nothing. Quiet.

Then out of the trees they came. Two drones flew at them like screaming eagles, firearm barrels pointing toward them like bayonets. Bullets strafed the water on either side of the boat as the drones passed, and Ramsey grabbed the wheel and swerved away from the dock and toward the open lake.

The drones had disappeared but he knew they'd be back. He turned on the radio, to frequency sixteen, used for emergencies, and said they had a man who had been shot on board and we're being chased. No answer.

Ramsey sped back toward the boathouse. It would take at least eight minutes to get back at full speed. Hoken was holding Hughes, who was losing a lot of blood and was in shock. He kept mumbling "Not again, not again."

"Look," she shouted, pointing off the starboard side into the distance. The drones were coming in about fifteen feet off the water.

Ramsey shouted into the radio again. No answer. Not a lot of boat activity in November, so maybe the police were somewhere else. Bad timing. Thinking, he turned the frequency back to twenty-five, just in time to hear someone shout "Kappa, engage!"

"Starfucker," Ramsey shouted. "Disengage. Repeat. Disengage. We have a wounded man here."

Nothing. He looked up and in came the drones off the starboard side. At the last minute, just as the bullets started strafing, he swerved the boat toward them, absorbing the bullets in the front seating pads and windshield, which shattered. The drones sped past and down over the trees on the north coast.

Ramsey could see the boathouse now. "Starfucker, do you hear me?" Ramsey shouted. Nothing.

He turned back to sixteen in time to hear a local police dispatcher trying to reach him.

"Where are you?" she said.

"He gave her the name of the boathouse and said they were racing toward it, pursued by flying objects shooting at them."

She said a squad car would be there in five minutes. Ramsey didn't have five minutes. The drones had reappeared and were coming rapidly up from behind.

This time they were one foot off the lake. Ramsey knew if they fired at that level, they'd hit the twin engines. He was a quarter mile from the boathouse.

Ramsey set the boat on autopilot and leaped down into the stern well, where Hoken was cradling Hughes' head.

"We have to jump."

"What?" she screamed, turning her head and seeing the drones approaching. She understood in a second.

Together they grabbed Hughes and leaped up toward the rail. The last thing Hoken saw as she and the boy and Ramsey tumbled into the water was the boathouse manager on his dock, shooting indiscriminately toward them and the boat with his shotgun.

Ramsey and Hoken wrestled to keep Hughes' head above water and as they surfaced, the drones flew inches over their heads, shooting at the twin engines. Three seconds later, the boat pitched to the right, just missing the dock, and the boat manager, hit another dock and blew up, sending a towering pillar of flame and black smoke into the sky.

The manager was blown off the dock but was standing in shoulder-high water. Ramsey had Hughes under his arm and was paddling in, followed by Hoken.

The boat manager helped haul Hughes in.

"What was that you said about us being safe?" he said to Ramsey as they tumbled onto shore.

Chapter 14

President McHenry was apoplectic. He shouted at Pastor and Forrester as they tried to keep him ahead of the news.

"What are you people doing? Things are blowing up all around us. We need coordination. Are you even talking to one another?"

Forrester looked at Pastor, who looked down.

"Sir, events are moving fast, but we're tracking and working with local governments as we can," Forrester said. "We just got word of another shooting at a college game in Columbia, Missouri. That's three shootings, a drone attack, and a bomb so far."

"Sir, we need to dust off the old Al Qaida plans," Pastor interrupted.

"What are you talking about?" McHenry said.

"Back when President Bush was in charge, after 9/11, Vice President Cheney approved a plan for this type of scenario. Remember, they landed every plane in the country in under two hours that morning. It was an amazing feat. Cheney kept the details, and more, in a secret plan to be activated if ever Al Qaida – or anybody – attacked in multiple areas simultaneously again. Bush approved it."

"Well, where is it, and what does it call for?"

Pastor looked at Forrester, then at the rest of the cabinet, then at the President.

"Martial law, sir."

"Goddammit, Robert, I told you we're not going to do that. This is America, not Myanmar. I won't be the president that turns on the people. Never."

Pastor pulled his briefcase out from beside his chair, put it on the table, snapped it open, and withdrew a sheath of papers. He stood and walked them over to the president.

"Here it is, sir. I grabbed it on my way here after hearing about the attacks. It was only known in a small circle in the Bush cabinet at the time, but the plans are all there. A coded message would go out to the armed forces across the country, and efforts to secure vital installations and enforce a nationwide curfew would be enacted within hours."

McHenry scanned it, growing redder with each page.

"What the fuck is this," he finally said. *Fucking Cheney*, he thought. "This footnote said part of this was drawn from the effort by the German Democratic Republic in East Berlin to build the Berlin Wall in 1961?"

"They built it virtually overnight, sir," Pastor said calmly. "The Chinese have done similar things. It takes coordination, but the blueprint is here."

"So now we're the Chinese and the goddam Russians and East Germans," McHenry shouted.

"Bomb blast in Waco," Forrester said casually. "This one looks big. We also have reports of immigrants streaming across the Mexican border by the hundreds.

Border guards are shooting at them, and in some cases, they are shooting back."

"If we lose control of the border, sir, things could really escalate quickly," Forrester said.

"Listen, sir. I spent my career in the military. I was in Iraq," Pastor said. "In Fallujah, with my unit. I've seen what happens when there is no plan. It's every man for himself and his buddies. We can't have that here."

Forrester looked up and frowned. McHenry sighed. "Get me the joint chiefs of staff, and prepare a line to the 50 state governors. We will at least begin to prepare."

Just then, all heads turned as an aide turned up the TV screen in the corner. CNN headlines were reporting a blast at Pike's Place Fish Market in Seattle. A big one.

***

Starks roared out of his garage in his black Porsche Cayenne and turned toward Reno. He was furious. Just as he was about to activate phase two, he had been compromised. He had no one to blame but himself. He had loved that house. Perhaps when this was over, he could find a way to reclaim it.

For now, he had his computer, his phones, his weapons, his drone controls, and most important, more than $3 million in cash. If need be, he could be out of the country in less than three hours. But now he was heading to a secure location in the penthouse of one of his casinos, to prepare for phase two, the invasion.

Children of the Light Horse, some 25,000 militiamen and women in seven locations around the country, had been put on call the day before Thanksgiving, and would be activated over the weekend to secure vital locations in their areas. Just two more triggers remained before activation: the storming of Las Vegas, and the declaration of martial law by an unwitting president.

Starks had contacts in both places. In Vegas, Randy Chatham could be counted on to lead his troops directly into a firefight. As they marched down the Strip, Starks could tip off police just in time for them to respond with enough force to ensure a nationally televised, made-for-America war between authorities and patriots. The public reaction would handle the rest.

In DC, it was a bit more complicated. He had confidence in Jackknife, his old marine buddy, who had rescued him that day in Fallujah. But ever since Jackknife had moved into the upper echelon of security clearance, and into the Presidential circle, he had been harder to reach unless at approved times.

Jackknife had promised he'd convince the president to declare martial law. He had dusted off the old Bush-Cheney plan and added some modern, digital advancements, such as drones, GPS tracking, and artificial intelligence. Much of the work would be achieved simply by shutting down power grids. Starks would handle the rest. By the time McHenry realized Homeland Security was tied into the revolution, it would be too late.

He headed toward the Bonanza Resort and Spa Casino. His next call with Jackknife was set for forty minutes from now. Just enough time to get Chatham and his gang in motion. But before that, he needed to brief Johnson.

***

"Where are you?" Johnson said calmly into his latest silver and gold burner. "I've tried you three times. Seems like all is playing out as planned. I just saw the Pike Place explosion on CNN."

"Use this number from now on. That phone was compromised. Small setback but everything is still in place. I'm heading to the Bonanza for the rest. Vegas is poised to go. Will reach out when all the units have been activated. In the meantime, enjoy the show."

Johnson put down the phone and sat back in his home office in Evergreen, Colo., and gazed at the early snow on the treetops outside his window. He had steadily been building short positions in the major equity markets over the last few weeks, using off-shore accounts tied to a half dozen financial institutions in Europe and Asia so that nobody could track the size of his trade.

The New York Stock Exchange had still been open when the first few attacks made the news that morning, and stocks had promptly plummeted. The Dow Jones industrial average fell 400 points, and the S&P 500 was down about 1.5% as well. With three days of chaos between the mid-day, holiday close on Friday and the opening of global markets on Monday, sufficient panic would ensue about the stability of the U.S. to create one of the great selloffs in history, akin to 1929, 1987, or even the pandemic-induced crash of 2020.

With luck, Johnson would be $25 billion richer in a week, even as he was seen as a national hero for quelling the unrest and establishing order with his teams. If Starks failed, he had deniability, and would still have the money.

Jackknife was the key. The president must declare martial law for any of this to work. The next twenty-four hours would decide the fate of a nation, that had idolized its own gun-toting prowess for two centuries, and would now face the inevitable consequence of its misunderstanding of its own Constitution.

Johnson whistled again. He loved America.

***

Hoken and Ramsey were still half-soaked, leaning against the rental car and finishing de-briefing the local police about the boat explosion. There was no evidence of any drones, but Hughes had clearly been shot. He had been taken away in an ambulance, and it looked like he would survive.

The police would pay a visit to the house on the lake, but Ramsey knew it would be empty, along with any evidence. *Where would Starfucker go from here*, he thought to himself. *Other than another Tahoe residence, or down the hill into Sacramento, it would have to be back to Reno. After all, it was listed in the Miller documents. But where to start?*

Ramsey took out his phone and Googled popular Reno destinations. Not surprisingly, they were all casinos: Peppermill, Atlantis, Bonanza, Grand Sierra. All resorts with, golf, sun, and betting. Hoken came up behind him and put her head on his shoulder. "What now?"

"I still think we're close. Guess we head back toward Reno-Tahoe International and rethink our steps."

Hoken glanced at his phone. She pursed her lips and frowned, then pointed. "That place."

"What?" Ramsey said.

"Bonanza. Wasn't that one of the code names in Miller's hard drive?"

Ramsey flicked through his phone for a minute. "I thought it had to do with this area, on the east side of the lake. "This is where the show was supposed to be."

"What show?" Hoken looked up.

"Bonanza. Didn't you ever…" Ramsey stopped himself. She was way too young. "A TV show long ago."

"Well, it's also a casino resort." She looked up at him smiling. "Want to try our luck?"

***

Randy was up early that Friday morning. Military men such as himself, he thought, always got up with the sun. He cleaned his guns, inspected his hunting knife, and shook the dust off his bullet-proof vest.

The plans he had been given were simple. They would start out by McCarran International Airport on the South side of the Strip. A small detachment would attack the

149

main terminal, emerging from the car rental and short-term parking garages across the street. With the airport paralyzed, and police called in to address the chaos, Randy and his squad would be open to start moving up the Strip to the north, past the Mandalay Bay Hotel and the MGM, along by the famous 20-story fountains of the Bellagio Hotel, and up toward the downtown area.

His instructions were simply to clear out the Strip, fire over people's heads, and cause mass panic as they ran inside. He expected little resistance initially but knew that as they made their way north, the police would mount some sort of counterattack, or at least erect a barrier. His plan was to move his squad as quickly as possible. He had taken that assignment for himself, directing the two other squads that had met them in Henderson to deal with the airport or to spread out in key areas as backup when his main column started taking fire.

The Colonel had told him a small fleet of drones would provide air cover.

Randy had waited for this all his life. Starfucker had told him his mission would expose the evil U.S. government for what it truly was and send a signal that the people of the United States would not be dictated to. If successful, he imagined he would inherit a larger brigade for future missions.

At no time did he consider whether he and his men were being sacrificed as part of a larger disruption plan.

Tom Rooney, a gap-toothed car mechanic with a patch over one eye, came strutting into the makeshift compound Randy had set up around his truck. From above, the entire area just looked like a big tailgate party. Something that might occur on any football weekend ahead of the Raiders game off the Strip.

"Getting close," Rooney said, his smile exposing his desire to start shooting people.

"Yep, expect the orders in about two hours. Gun checks complete?"

"Yeah. Some guys getting a little nervous, but I'll handle them. No room for chickenshits on a battlefield."

Randy looked up at him. Sweat dripped from his chin. It was approaching noon and the temperature was already above 100 in November.

"When the sun goes down today, you and I will be national heroes, Tom," he said, sending a gob of spit about six feet to the left. "It's about time somebody does something to send those East Coast faggots a message."

***

Starks parked his Cayenne in his VIP space below the Bonanza and walked quickly over to the private elevator that would take him to his penthouse control room. He had built it out to replicate the control room at the lake house, just in case he needed an auxiliary. The elevator responded only to his card and other elevators in the hotel resort didn't even include his penthouse on their electronic boards.

The door opened on the 48th floor and he walked quickly down a hall, past the emergency exit stairs to the roof and the floors below, pressed his hand on the door activation monitor, and entered. Inside, he looked past the commanding view of the snow-packed Sierras and went straight to his control panels.

Starks logged in and assessed the situation. Chatham was in position in Vegas and awaiting his signal. The other seven operation chiefs had already checked in: Driggs, Lawrence, Roanoke, Tuscaloosa, Pensacola, El Paso, and even the backup in Kenosha. All ready to move on local installations to seize control. In El Paso, it was the border, which was currently wide open as migrants streamed in from Mexico. In Pensacola, it was the local air force base.

Starks glanced over at CNN. The chaos at Pike's Market and the border openings in Texas were on a split screen, as headlines streamed across the bottom about the other bombings and shootings. He sent the code to the operation leaders to prepare to advance, then called Chatham from a protected landline.

"Time to make history, Randy. Commence. Starfucker out."

Starks put down the phone and pushed his swivel chair across the transom to another bank of computers. He sent another encrypted message to an address outside of Washington D.C., an empty military office on the 21st floor of a tower along the Potomac River in Alexandria, Va.

This was his failsafe strategy. A small team of three, handpicked by Jackknife, sat at terminals overlooking the Pentagon on one side of the floor and the Capitol on the other. From there, they activated the drones in all seven locations and programmed them to gather from hundreds of miles around and prepare to back up the militias as they advanced. Only Starks could deactivate them once they had been set in motion.

More than 25,000 drones, the largest drone air force in American history, powered up simultaneously around the country, and began to maneuver toward their destinations. They included 175 drones specifically picked from Roanoke to move their way toward the Capitol and the White House.

Starks knew there was no better way to generate panic and action at the top than by including them in the attack, showing them what they were up against.

Once the battle of Vegas was on TV screens, he would send a last secure text message to Johnson, who would then let the President know that his team had volunteered to secure the nation over the weekend and that orders were being carried out.

Johnson would make sure to distance himself, only saying that he regarded it as a patriotic duty to do his part to keep the country safe. By the time he realized, late Friday night or Saturday morning, that the actual plan was for the militia to take over from the military, not support them, it would be too late. Children of the Light Horse would be in charge.

Johnson's cover would be blown, and the full force of American intelligence would come raining down on his head before lunchtime tomorrow. Starks, meanwhile, would cut off contact and direct operations from a new perch in an undisclosed location, unknown to Johnson.

It was perfect. Once in control, he would use his casino channels to transfer up to $2 billion to an offshore market in the Caribbean, where he hoped to be by Tuesday. Starks had one more move to make. He sent an encrypted email to a source at the Las Vegas police department, warning of an imminent invasion of the Strip.

Operation Pigskin had begun.

Chapter 15

Hoken and Ramsey parked their car across the street from the Bonanza in public parking and made their way across the thoroughfare to the casino entrance. He held her hand as they crossed the street. Fortunately, there were no weapons checks or metal detectors. Nevada was a gun state, and open carry had long been enshrined in local laws, including inside casinos.

Hoken looked around as they walked down a purple neon corridor and were greeted with the dinging and ringing of the slot machines and the cool, manufactured air of an oxygen-pumped casino. Even by Nevada standards, the Bonanza was huge. More than 165,000 square feet of slots, blackjack tables, craps, and roulette, a sportsbook, and restaurants and bars galore.

Ramsey knew they were on camera the minute they walked in, but he figured if they kept their composure and just looked like any other over-stimulated couple in the casino, they would escape detection, perhaps for long enough to find out where Starks was located.

***

All casinos had advanced security staffs and control rooms to monitor gamblers, with cameras embedded in the ceilings and on the walls. Ramsey knew better than to glance around for them. They were there.

He figured the control room would be close, perhaps on the second floor. Perhaps in the basement. He and Hoken walked slowly, eyeing the tables like interested gamblers. He stopped at one blackjack table and put down $50 for a handful of red, $5 chips. He gave four to Hoken, who sat down and placed two on the table. Ten, four, hit, nine. Lose. She laid the other two chips down. Jack, queen. Hold. Dealer queen. Ace. Lose.

Hoken looked up at Ramsey. "That was quick."

"That's why I try to avoid these places," he said.

She stood up and they walked toward the hotel lobby and the bank of elevators. Hoken hit the basement, and down they went. They walked down a corridor into what looked like the beginnings of the kitchen. It was massive. Inside, workers hurried about, preparing room service meals and salad bars for the restaurants.

"Excuse me," Ramsey said to one of the more senior ones. "I'm looking for the security department."

The chef eyed him, then gave Hoken the up and down. "Just got robbed in the parking lot," he said, pulling at his pockets as if empty.

The chef pointed them toward another corridor. "Cien yardas," he said. "One hundred yards."

Hoken and Ramsey made their way down the corridor and came to an official red door with a light above and a security sign. Locked. They waited a few minutes until someone came by and tapped his security card on the door.

After he walked, in, Ramsey grabbed the door and they quickly stepped inside.

"Excuse me, you can't be in here," the guard said, turning around and realizing his mistake.

"I'm sorry, they told me to come here," Ramsey said, introducing doubt into the conversation and then advancing quickly toward him as Hoken looked around. "We were robbed in the parking lot and the guard upstairs said to come to report it."

"That is a job for the police."

"I am the police," Ramsey said, flashing his badge quickly. "Off duty. Our car was broken into. Can you please get your manager? I want to look at the tape."

"Wait here," he said, and turned around. It was the break they needed. In the next four minutes, each of them scanned the room as quickly as possible. Your usual monitors on the gaming tables, parking lot, hotel entrances, and rotating video of hallways. Ramsey noticed one stable feed though, peaking down a dark corridor with a green door at the end. That's the one, he figured. But where? He took out his camera and snapped a photo of it.

"Hey, no pictures," someone approaching said.

"Sorry, I was looking to see if I had a photo of my busted side window, but I don't."

"I'm the duty manager. I'm sorry, you, officer, but you'll need to contact the LVMPD first, then we can go over the tape with them."

"Damn it," Ramsey said. "This is only the second day of our vacation."

"Sorry sir, now if you'll please leave."

Ramsey and Hoken went back out into the corridor. They walked to the elevators again and got in. Ramsey glanced at his camera. He enlarged the photo. Down near the green door was another door on the side, with an Exit to Roof sign. Bingo. He hit the button for the top floor.

***

McCarran International Airport was on heightened security that morning, as were all airports nationwide given the chaos unfolding across the country. But it was still open, and excited travelers, pumped with a cocktail or two on the plane, streamed out toward the taxi lines, as hungover, somewhat more broke than before revelers emerged from cabs with their bags and slouched their way toward check-in.

Graham Hughes, bandage on his shoulder, was being wheeled across the pedestrian walkway by his brother, Phil, after a puddle-jump from Reno to recuperate from the lake shooting for a week.

"You won't believe how much has happened since I last saw you, big bro," said Hughes. "It has changed my perspective. I'm ready to become part of the solution." Phil nodded. He had some work to do to fix his brother's head.

The brothers were crossing the pedestrian walkway and headed toward the rental car buses when they first saw what looked like a military unit approaching from the dark garage.

Hughes' first thought was it must be some parade, or else a group called to add security to the airport. As they emerged, less than 10 yards away, they opened fire, shooting above the Hughes brothers' heads as they dove for the ground, and hurling smoke bombs toward the airport entrance.

"You got to be fucking kidding me," Hughes shouted as he writhed on the ground. His brother, meanwhile, had taken out his pistol and was covering Hughes until it became clear the armed figures had already passed them and were entering the airport. He fired a shot into the airport doors, hitting a bystander trying to escape the mayhem in the leg.

"Goddammit," Hughes shouted as he struggled to get up. His brother ran toward the airport, and he followed him inside, unarmed and clutching his shoulder.

Suddenly, the terminal erupted in chaos. Passengers ran in every direction, dropping their bags and diving for cover as the group entered the main terminal and split in two directions, heading for security. They simply overwhelmed the guards, who could only manage to duck behind counters and call for reinforcements.

Chatham waited until he heard the first sirens of police and fire engines heading toward the airport. Then he gave the signal to his men.

Four RVs advanced up the strip and swung together to form a blockage at the intersection in front of the MGM Grand, halting all traffic. Militia men emerged from the vehicles and began firing into the air. From both sides of the street, they were met by teams of other militiamen, and began a slow walk up the famous broad Strip, shooting over the heads of terrified tourists and into the windows of cars, buses, and hotels on either side.

One man, holding a half-yard glass full of blue alcohol, handed it to the girl next to him and took out his gun, and began firing back. A barrage of bullets sliced through him and the girl, who was still holding the drink as she fell.

Three more armed civilians ducked behind fences and cement plant holders and started firing back as well. One militiaman fell, and the unit began to splinter as it made its way up the Strip.

Casino lobbies were chaos as people fleeing inside were met by guards making their way outside. A local news truck halfway down the strip, immediately broadcast the scene to the studio, as social media began to fill with viral posts about shootings in Vegas.

Back at the airport, the militias had made it to the security gates and were in a firefight with the TSA, which was badly under-armed. Off-duty soldiers in the terminals reached for their weapons and made their way back to security to try to help until the police could get there.

But the police were already in full operation. A tip had come just minutes before the assault, giving them enough time to alert passing units, which had arrived just as the militiamen were entering the terminal. Soon, the militias were pinched between TSA officers providing cover fire and police units firing from behind. An ATF unit was coming up the ramp.

Hughes staggered inside but couldn't find his brother, who had joined the firefight. He crouched down instinctively, hoping to reduce his target. On the ground, he found a gun, a Luger, next to the body of what looked like one of the militiamen. Hughes grabbed it from the nose, not sure what to do.

The militia fought hard, but as soon as the ATF arrived it was clear they were fighting a losing battle. Some started to surrender. Others fought to the end. One-man, red bandana wrapped around his head, seeing there was no way out, grabbed a young child out of his mother's arms.

"No," she screamed, but he swiped at her with his pistol and then put it to the boy's head, moving back to the wall down the hallway as the ATF began to gather and point their weapons at him.

Slowly he backed, dragging the boy, a maniacal smile on his face, until he turned a corner and looked for an escape route.

He hadn't time to look up before a bullet tour half his face off. The boy screamed and fell to the floor. The militiamen dropped like a stone. The ATF ran up. Standing in front of them, holding his shoulder and clinging to the gun, was Graham Hughes.

"Put the gun down," the police said. "He dropped it and fell to the ground."

"Did I get him?" he asked no one in particular.

"You got him, now stay down."

Hughes looked at the ground. Five yards away, he watched the assailant bleeding out, his eyes still looking for an escape. Hughes threw up. This was not how he expected revenge to feel.

***

Back on the Strip, Chatham breathed the smoke from the firearms and smiled. He'd never had such fun. People scattered before him, with many down and blood everywhere. He walked up the Strip straight as an arrow, pointing his gun and firing at anybody he could find. Orders were to fire above heads, but Chatham couldn't help himself.

Suddenly, he looked ahead 100 yards to what appeared to be a small army assembling, and a helicopter coming from directly behind them.

How did the police assemble so quickly, he thought? Just then, eight drones in formation soared 10 feet above his head, firing straight at the helicopter. The copter pitched to one side and blew up just as it hit the ground, taking out two empty taxi cabs. The drones split into groups of four and soared off to each side, ready to come around again when called upon.

Chatham whooped and hollered as he began firing again.

At the Bonanza in Reno, Starks smiled as he watched the action from one of the drone cameras, and from the TV feed being broadcast through CNN. He hadn't told the police there would be drones.

He checked his watch. By now the other units would be mobilizing around the country. In about an hour, as social media exploded with running battles in the streets across the nation, Jackknife would shut down parts of the national grid with an encrypted virus from one of his Homeland, elite hacker teams.

As darkness began to descend on the East Coast, President McHenry would be forced to declare martial law. Starks sat back and allowed himself the luxury of a small Cohiba cigar. Nothing to do now but watch.

As he lit the match, he heard a small explosion.

***

Ramsey and Hoken had made it to the top floor, but saw no green door. Just hotel rooms. They scrambled into the emergency stairwell to climb to the roof, and halfway up, they saw the green door.

"There's another floor," Ramsey whispered. It was not surprising. Casino hotels routinely played with floor numbers to make them seem more appealing to guests. Some with floors numbered sixty were actually only thirty stories high. Part of the magic of Vegas, Ramsey assumed.

He tried the door, but he knew it would be locked. They went up to the roof and looked over the side. No way to tell what was behind the window below, but they were lucky to find a locked-up window-washing unit about thirty yards away. Ramsey busted the lock with the butt of his gun and swung the aerial walkway over the edge. He played with the controls until he could figure out how to move it up and down, and sideways.

"Stay here," he said to Hoken.

"No way," she said, grabbing his arm. "The story is down there."

"Jesus, you reporters," he exclaimed. "Okay, here's the lever. Up. Down. Sideways."

Hoken was looking at her phone. "My god, there's a firefight on the Vegas Strip. At this rate, the army will be on the streets by nightfall."

Ramsey took a deep breath. "Okay, let's go."

The cop and the reporter descended slowly, and as they did, they could make out a room full of computers and monitors, and a figure on the other side. But the glaze on the windows was too much to make out much else.

Ramsey thought for a moment. "Man, am I ever out of my jurisdiction," he said to nobody in particular. Then he took out his firearm and pumped three blasts into the window.

Starks was stunned as the explosions shattered both the window and his celebration. He peered through the glass to see Ramsey leaping into the room. There was no alarm on the windows, so he was on his own.

He reached over to the main computer and typed a command, then he pulled his sidearm.

But Ramsey was on him like a hornet. The cop and the former marine tumbled over the chair and onto the ground underneath the monitors. Starks, on the bottom, shot a knee up into Ramsey's groin and used all his shoulder strength to bang Ramsey's head against the desk.

Ramsey groaned but held on, reaching for Starks' throat and tightening his grip. Starks punched out, and Ramsey released his grip, grabbing Stark's chain necklace and dog tag, and ripping them off as he rolled away. Starks reached for his firearm but Ramsey knocked it out of his hand and leaped on him again. Hoken watched the two men from the aerial walkway and contemplated the two-and-a-half-foot leap it would take to make it into the room. She hated heights, and tried not to look at the parking lot below.

Ramsey struggled to contain Starks, but the former marine was stronger, younger, and angrier. He rolled Ramsey onto the ground, spinning him onto his stomach, and reached up to grab his Swiss Army cigar lighter. He swung it high over his head, its tip aimed for the back of Ramsey's neck, when a massive jolt hit him in the right shoulder, knocking him back against the console.

Hoken stood there with the pistol Ramsey had given her. Those old shooting lessons in Door County had come in handy after all.

Starks stared at her in disbelief. Here he was again. Wounded. But this time with no Jackknife around to help him. He was on his own. But he had his orders. He reached up with his left hand and yanked the laptop monitor from the desk and down on top of him. He punched the enter button, shoved the monitor off his body, and smiled as he turned and rushed toward Hoken, screaming.

Hoken tried to step to the side, but he was coming in low and fast. She pulled the trigger again, spinning Starks around and causing him to lose his footing. He slid through the broken glass off the edge of window, but managed to grab hold of the walkway and wrap his arm around it.

He hung there, rasping, looking up at Hoken. But there was no anger in his eyes. Instead, almost a look of triumph. In his last act, he had switched the drones to autonomous mode, programmed with orders to shoot at any and all heat-producing forms, i.e., all humans. And he had programmed two units with specific targets – President McHenry and Ginny Robinson.

If he couldn't lie on a beach in the Caribbean smoking Cohibas, at least he would change the world. He never liked the beach anyway.

His eyes smiled as he looked at Hoken one last time.

"Semper Fi," he said, as he let go of the handrail and fell into the hot Vegas sky.

***

Hoken watched in horror as Starks fell away, then turned to Ramsey, who was struggling to stand up.

"Are you okay?" she said.

"Yes, the guy had a helluva quick knee."

They both knew they only had so much time before security figured out something was wrong up there. They turned to the control panels but were caught off guard by the scenes from Vegas.

Chapter 16

Chatham smiled as he emptied his Colt AR-15 Sporter into the streets before him. He stepped through the wreckage of the police chopper and started aiming up toward the hotels on either side of the Strip: Paris, Bellagio, Venetian. He saw people ducking down into the famous fountain outside the Bellagio, some of them returning fire, and let go of a barrage of bullets in their general direction.

He turned to see his unit moving forward; a bit broken but still in some sloppy formation, and he watched as three more helicopters approached, guns firing. He looked back for his drone cover and saw them in the sky, swooping down from the clouds into a tight group, eight across and fifteen feet off the ground, heading toward the police.

Suddenly, Chatham's face turned pale. The drones slid lower and came right up the back of his men, blasting through them before they even knew where the fire was coming from. Half of his unit fell in unison. The drones then slid apart and soared upward again, only to turn individually and point back down at – everyone. Police, bystanders, the media truck. The firefight had become a shooting gallery for the drones.

Chatham saw the police switch their attention to firing at the drones. Bystanders too. He stood, mouth agape, trying to understand what had happened to his cover. This was supposed to be his victory against an oppressive government. A win for gun rights and the American people who carried them.

Instead, the guns had turned against him. And everybody. The enemy was now the very weapons he had fought so hard his whole life to hang on to. They had betrayed him. Where was Starfucker? How could this happen?

Chatham turned to see a single drone above him, about sixty feet. It executed a mid-air flip and dove straight down at him. He raised his rifle and blew it out of the sky, leaping onto the side of the fountain, which had just started its operatic sky dance. Standing alone and screaming obscenities known only to himself, Chatham fired through the fountain and what he thought was another drone. Then another.

The waters shot up eleven stories, swaying as the music hit a crescendo, accompanied by great slapping sounds as the water fell back to the fountain, as if in applause for him. He took out another drone. Then a third. He slipped into the fountain and emerged soaking wet, screaming for backup as the fountain subsided.

Then he looked up, just as the spray dissolved, to see them, rippling just above the tiny waves as they raced toward him in unison—the enemy he had never even thought about.

He raised his waterlogged rifle to shoot but was sliced entirely in half before he could pull the trigger. His face, slamming into the cool, bloody water, still filled with hate.

***

President McHenry checked his tie and prepared to go on the air. It was now dark on the East Coast, and he was starting to get reports of power outages in New York, Atlanta, and Miami. The images from his news screens were appalling. In the studio with him but outside camera view were Pastor and Forrester.

The last thing he had done before walking into the room was to call Ginny Robinson at her home in Marin County. It was a difficult conversation.

"I'm going to have to call martial law, Ginny. The situation is out of control. There are militias marching in Idaho, Wisconsin, New Hampshire, Kansas, and Montana. We're hearing of copycat drone strikes across the country now. And have you seen the goddam fighting in Vegas?"

"Mr. President, Tom, with all due respect, you can't undo this once it is done. We are not Turkey or Myanmar. Do you know what that would trigger? For our allies? For the financial markets? For our Democracy itself?"

"It's been discussed before," he said. "Bush and Cheney had a full plan. They just never executed it. I don't see any other way around this. We're starting to hear reports even of drones firing indiscriminately into the crowds. We don't even really know what we're up against. We're under attack."

"I've already spoken with all relevant congressional leaders, as well as Pastor and Forrester. They are behind it. Once we get things calmed down, then we can begin an orderly return to normal. Hopefully in time for your inauguration, but I can't promise it. Right now, we have to stop the shooting."

Robinson put down the phone and put her head in her hands. How had it come to this? The unthinkable. Suddenly, a nation with more than three hundred million firearms in circulation was taking up arms against each other. She thought of past mass shootings of children. How each time the cause against guns had been raised, and how each time it was ignored. People had been arming themselves for the best part of thirty years, preparing for this day. Now it had come.

She prepared to make her own speech on the airwaves. She would support McHenry but underscore that this was a temporary solution. The suspension of a two hundred and fifty-year-old democracy. She didn't look forward to the next twenty-four hours.

She raised her head suddenly, hearing popping sounds. She instinctively ducked behind her desk as the windows above her shattered in a hail of bullets. Her security raced into the room, guns drawn, in time to see two drones circling back above the brown Marin County hills. They grabbed Robinson and raced her downstairs to an improvised secure location, walkie-talkies squawking for support.

"Ladyhawk under attack," went the message, using Robinson's proposed presidential code name for the first time.

McHenry didn't hear about it right away. He had problems of his own. The minute he hung up with Robinson, his own Secret Service had rushed into the studio and grabbed him, Pastor, and Forrester, and moved them into the secure bunker at Camp David. A small fleet of drones had been spotted circling the White House, and now there were reports of them buzzing Camp David.

"What about my broadcast?" McHenry shouted.

"Mr. President, we can move the equipment into the bunker here for it," Pastor said.

"I can't broadcast from a goddam bunker. Like I'm cowering in fear somewhere. Take care of these fuckers and get me back to the studio."

***

Hoken and Ramsey stared at the scenes in Vegas and couldn't believe their eyes. Not just the firefight, but that it appeared the drones were firing at every living thing.

"Whose side are they on?" Hoken said, grabbing Ramsey's arm.

"I never thought I'd see anything like this," Ramsey said, pulling his pistol out and looking at it. "We are armed to the teeth, but don't know who the enemy is."

Television headlines began to flash that President McHenry was about to address the nation. That he would call martial law and activate the military.

"It's another Civil War," he said.

They looked at Starks' computer. A list of numbers flashed up on one of the open windows, with common area codes. Denver. Vegas. Washington DC.

"Washington? That wasn't one of the militia centers. Can you track it?" Hoken said.

"Looks like a secure number, but use his computer to text it," he said.

Hoken texted the number.

"Trouble here. What's your status?" the text read, under the Starfucker account.

They waited. Writing coming.

"Almost there. But the fuckers are firing at everyone. What did you do?" came the response, from an account called Jackknife.

Ramsey and Hoken breathed deeply. Almost there? Martial law? Firing at everyone?

Hoken went on her computer. Who was Jackknife? She accessed Starks' bio. His past in the Marines. Fallujah. Something about being injured there. Purple heart. Battlefield bravery. She kept looking. No names. She went into his photos and scanned for… she didn't know what.

She found a few old military photos, but she could barely make out Starks, much less anyone else. She scanned the names but nothing clicked.

Hoken flipped through a couple of later photos. Tahoe. Boat. Golf buddies. Wait, this one looked familiar. She looked harder. Suddenly, she went back to the military photos. A bunch of guys in their young twenties on patrol. Who was the guy in the floppy hat? That was the same guy. Bobby the J, read the handwritten caption. Bobby the J? The Jackknife.? She looked again at his face under the shadow of the hat, then scrolled back to the golfing photo, maybe five or six years ago. Bobby. That was Robert Pastor—the chief of Homeland Security.

"Oh fuck," she shouted.

Hoken had interviewed Pastor a year ago when the President had come through Chicago. He was the highest-ranking official the White House could put up, and he would be up to his neck in these attacks right now, she could imagine.

Could Pastor be Jackknife? She quickly showed Ramsey, who was on the phone with the FBI, trying to figure out how to deactivate the drones.

Ramsey stopped talking in mid-sentence. His face turned white as he looked at Hoken.

"He could convince the President to declare martial law," he said in a hoarse voice. They looked at another TV screen. The press conference had been delayed. CNN anchors were debating the prospects of martial law as they waited for word when the presser would start again.

The U.S. had used martial law before, but only locally and in times of great crisis. The Great Chicago Fire of 1871. The San Francisco earthquake of 1906. Race riots in the 1920s in Nebraska. It had never been declared for the entire country.

"We have to reach the President," Ramsey said.

Hoken searched her contacts for the White House press office. She hit the number. It rang five times before a harried staffer answered.

"We'll have a statement as soon as we can," she barked before Hoken could even introduce herself.

"Wait, I'm not looking for a statement. I'm Lindsey Hoken from WBBM in Chicago. I have to reach the President. We have a vital message for him about one of his team members."

"What it is?" the staffer asked.

"I need to speak to him," Hoken said.

"Get in line," the staffer said and hung up. Hoken dialed back but no answer this time. Damn.

She looked up at Ramsey, who was screaming into his phone trying to get Bledsoe at the FBI. She glanced over to CNN. The battle in Vegas was in full swing, but now it was mostly local police and militia together trying to survive the drone assault. Smoke filled the strip and it was difficult to see who was who. On split screens, the video showed militia marching across the country. Lawrence, NH. Driggs, Idaho. Kenosha, Wis. Fredericksburg, Virginia. Less than half an hour from the White House.

Flaming barricades were being set up on key highways in and out of major cities. Homeowners across the country raced to unlock their firearms and get their families inside houses. Neighborhood watch groups quickly became armed checkpoints, as looters ravaged through towns, breaking windows and setting fires as they raced in and out of storefronts.

Suddenly, an idea. Hoken went back into her phone, scrolling furiously. There it was. Ginny Robinson's private phone number. She hit the link and took a deep breath.

"Who's this?" said the President-Elect.

Chapter 17

President McHenry walked back into the TV studio with Pastor and Forrester in tow. The Secret Service had taken care of the first drones, though there were reports of more on the way. The Air Force had been scrambled to protect Camp David. McHenry only needed ten minutes to broadcast to the nation and then he would get back down to the bunker.

Secret servicemen looked nervously out of windows, guns drawn, as McHenry approached the podium.

His phone beeped. He glanced down. Robinson.

"Here, hold this," he said to Forrester. I can talk with her later.

Forrester grabbed the phone and let the call die. She was about to put it in her pocket when it beeped again. She hit hang up and was looking for the button to turn it off when it beeped again. She hit connect and lifted the handset to her right ear.

"Madam President-Elect, we're just about to... what?"

She looked up at Pastor, who was staring back at her from across the room. The broadcast light went on.

"My fellow Americans," President McHenry began.

Forrester sprinted toward him. Suddenly, the video picture lurched to the left and blinked out.

***

Hoken looked at the dark screen and wondered if Forrester had stopped the President in time. What was Pastor's role in this? And why?

She didn't have time to think about it. Ramsey was now sharing Starks' computer screen with Bledsoe and other FBI tech agents, who were frantically trying to search for a trigger or password that might stop the drones. Something had programmed them to shoot at anything warm that moved. Humans. Dogs. Even birds. The result was a cross-country shootout the likes of which had never been seen before.

Machines against man. The doomsday scenario of a thousand science fiction books. Turns out guns do kill people.

Global leaders stared aghast at their television screens as America began to effectively break apart into violent chaos. The spontaneous combustion of a two hundred and fifty-year-old democracy. The greatest experiment in social freedom ever attempted now appeared doomed in the span of one murderous day.

She glanced at her phone again. Fifteen calls from her newsroom. Her job was the least of her worries right now. As Ramsey and the tech team searched through Starks' files, suddenly a banging on the door of the control room. Hotel security had found Starks' body amid broken glass in the back-parking lot and were trying to get in.

Hoken looked at Ramsey again. It had to be some easy digital instruction. He did it literally with one hand while fighting with Ramsey.

"Hurry, we only have a minute or so left," she yelled. Ramsey ignored her. Bledsoe and the team were looking for passwords but it would take forever to try them against the instructions, which they also hadn't found.

***

Robinson sped from her home in an armor-plated limousine. The Secret Service needed to get her to a safe location after the first drone attack, and it had chosen the West Coast branch of the Federal Reserve on Montgomery Street in San Francisco, about a half hour away over the Golden Gate Bridge. It had an underground vault that had been converted after 9/11 into a computer center in case of a terrorist attack from the skies again.

Robinson was back on the phone with Forrester. She had stopped McHenry from declaring martial law with seconds to spare, running across the studio and knocking the robotic camera onto its side. Pastor had been detained. They needed to figure out his network as quickly as possible, and Robinson was passing along what Hoken had told her about Starks, the control room in Reno, etc. Whether McHenry liked it or not, she was beginning to take charge.

As the limo descended from Marin's Robin Williams Tunnel down the headlands on Route 101 toward the Golden Gate, Robinson looked up at San Francisco in the distance. The familiar fog had begun to burn off, though there were still wispy remnants over the tops of the bridge.

Suddenly, the Secret Service car behind them got hit with crossfire and jumped over the guardrail and off the cliff. Robinson turned around quickly. Six drones had fired on it from behind when it came out of the tunnel. They were now following her. The officer in the passenger seat was on his phone, frantically calling for backup as they descended toward, and then onto the bridge.

Robinson looked to the left and saw more drones flying in from over the Bay, just past Alcatraz. On the right, four more were tracking the car from the other side, looking out over the gray Pacific Ocean.

Then, twenty-five feet above the traffic straight ahead, five drones flying straight toward them, gun barrels leveled at the windshield. Robinson's driver slammed on the brakes and swung the car to the right, absorbing the full blow of eighty bullets as they slammed into the back side of the armored car.

They were safe, but for how long?

"Go, go," Robinson shouted. They couldn't sit still. The driver swung the car back around and lit out for the city side of the bridge, but traffic was in chaos after the shooting. They banged past a couple of cars and started sprinting in the oncoming lane toward the toll plaza. Suddenly, more gunfire ripped into the street just in front of them. The drones were trying to drive them off the bridge.

Robinson thought of her family and how close she had come to the seat of power of the world's greatest

Democracy. What would happen to it now? Another line of drones appeared to the left. They arced up above the tower lines and started to dive toward the limousine. Ginny Robinson looked up through the skylight and held her breath.

***

Ramsey struggled with Starks' laptop as the FBI tried to break the code to freeze his drone order. Time was running out and they knew it.

Hoken looked over his shoulder, her hand on his back. He thought back to just two weeks beforehand when he hadn't even wanted this case. When Hoken was just another annoying reporter. When his career and his place in the world meant little to him, and he was just trying to get by.

Now he wanted nothing more than to live. To be with her. To find a way to stop this catastrophe that had been inflicted on his country by a group of disgruntled ex-Marines, who had convinced thousands to go to arms against their government.

Marines. Marines. Always faithful. To each other above all. What drove Starks and Pastor that would make them do this? Power? Money? But also, some sort of warped, misguided belief that they could build a better country their way. Always faithful.

As the hotel security began to shoot at the door, Hoken looked out the open window to see three drones hovering fifteen yards away, gun barrels leveled. Her hand tightened on Ramsey's shoulder.

Just then, one of the FBI hack squads broke through, turning up the control page Starks had used to activate the drones. At the top of it, in large red, capital letters, was a simple order: "Semper Fi." Always faithful.

Underneath it, a prompt for a ten-digit password. The digits were grayed out. Ramsey's mind was reeling as he tried to think how long it might take to try all alternatives.

"Help me, Bledsoe," he said.

"What about Starfucker?" the agent said.

Ramsey plugged in the word. Nothing.

"It has to be something close to him, something tied to the Marines," Bledsoe said. "Think, Ramsey!"

Ramsey could hear the buzzing of the drones now. The in-take of Hoken's breath. The metal scraping of the control room door being pushed off its hinges.

He looked frantically around the console table, and the floor, and there it was. Spark's dog tag. He slapped his left shoe on it and pulled it toward him. Grabbed it in his left hand and raised it to his eyes. A ten-digit number starting with the number 90, the year the first Gulf War started, and eight other digits to signify Sparks' unit.

Ramsey banged the numbers into the control page prompt and hit enter. It flashed green. A red abort button lit up. Ramsey slammed it with his left hand. Hoken turned her head just in time to see the drones drop from the sky.

***

President McHenry took Ginny Robinson's call this time. From his bunker at Camp David, he was monitoring reports pouring in from around the country that the drones had crashed and burned.

Talking from her bunker in San Francisco's Fed building, Robinson detailed her close call on the Golden Gate Bridge, which ended with three drones crashing harmlessly into the roof of her armored vehicle. No explosions.

"I'm sending Air Force One for you, Ginny. We need to appear in front of the country together as soon as possible. I'm not sure what happened to the drones, but we've got several major cities still in firefights. People are firing at anything that looks like a police car or military vehicle. We need to put a halt to this, but can't be too heavy-handed. That is what they wanted."

Robinson looked out her bullet-proof basement window up at the sidewalk. Feet were running back and forth. Nobody knew who was in charge. A large fire had been started nearby at Lotta's Fountain, where residents had gathered more than hundred years ago after the 1906 earthquake that destroyed the city.

"Where is Pastor?" she said.

"We've detained him, and both CIA and FBI are grilling him now. It appears to be some fucked up Marine thing left over from Iraq. I shudder to think what would have happened if we had actually declared martial law."

Robinson pondered the scenario and shut her eyes. She leaned forward in her chair, suddenly looking very much in control.

"Mr. President... Tom... we need to give the people what they want," Robinson said wearily.

"What? Anarchy?"

"No, their country. The thing each and every armed person out there right now is fighting for," she said.

"Ginny, we're on the brink of civil war. People can't tell the military from the militia. They are firing at everything."

"I know. If we crank up the military, this will take weeks to clean up, and we—you and I—might never live it down. We need the militias to come out of here this weekend with the feeling that they saved the country. It's always been their overriding purpose, not just to hoard guns.

"I don't think we have time for Air Force One. Let's rig up a two-shot where we can stand together from across the country, and thank the people for standing up and saving us all from the killer drones."

Two hours later, McHenry and Robinson broadcast to the nation, saying a terrorist menace had been stopped, in part thanks to the brave people of the United States who took up their arms and united as one."

Each knew it was bullshit, but it allowed police and military leaders to make contact with militia leaders and at least tone down the shooting. The fires, the looting, and the chaos would continue for days, but slowly people began to realize that the immediate threat had been stopped.

In Vegas, the carnage on The Strip had spread downtown. With the drones down, people began stripping the guns and ammunition off them and bursting into stores, casinos, and restaurants.

In Minneapolis, police took positions behind barricades and on top of buildings, but were instructed not to fire. A spark had been lit, and the fire needed to be contained but not smothered. Not just yet. Vehicles moved to contain the crowds into certain neighborhoods. Militia leaders began to call for a cease-fire, but as with any unregulated militia, order-taking was at best a long shot. Many militiamen couldn't resist firing into the crowds of rioters, both black and white.

In New York City, military aircraft crisscrossed the skies above Manhattan, in a show of force. But below, police and military also largely stuck to a plan of containment. In Boston, people began hanging American flags out their windows to support those who were trying to restore order, and to show those who weren't that they were not dangerous.

In Reno, Ramsey and Hoken sat at the back of Sparks' control room, holding each other and wondering if any of the other drones had stopped. Hotel security had breached the door, but Ramsey had calmed them down and told them the FBI was on its way, so not to touch anything.

Reports on the TV screens indicated that the drones had stopped shooting, or crashed, or disappeared, but the widespread social disorder was terrifying, with newscasts using "octo-boxes" of split screens to show city after city in flames as armed protesters, looters, and militias rampaged.

"What have we done to ourselves," Hoken whispered to nobody in particular. Ramsey grabbed her hand.

"Nobody ever said government "by the people" was going to be easy. But I never thought it would look like this."

Hoken's phone rang. Her newsroom again.

"Where have you been? The whole country is on fire," her editor said.

"I'm in Reno, and boy do I have a story for you."

"You better start filing ASAP or you can fucking stay out there," Joan Grantwell said.

"Better yet," Hoken offered, "Patch me in live in five minutes."

Hoken hung up. She stood and tucked her shirt in. Mussed her hair. It was only radio, but she had to put her professional face on. Ramsey said to leave him out of it, but she knew she couldn't. She smiled and walked to the window.

Where would she start? She took a deep breath and called back into the station.

"Yes, okay, ready. Hi Melissa. Lindsey Hoken coming to you from Reno, high up in the Bonanza casino, where police are investigating whether an ex-Marine with a history in the war in Iraq might have been connected to the deadly drones that have terrorized Americans for the last few weeks…"

***

Ramsey took position behind a tree and snapped his gun from its holster and held it to his chest, pointing to the sky. In the emerging dawn light, he could see the outlines of the house a hundred yards away. A light was on in the study, and curtains were partially drawn. He could almost make out the top of the head of the figure sitting in the chair, staring at its computer.

The FBI had been grateful for all his help on the case, and since he was out West anyway, had invited him to join the early-morning raid of Armand Johnson's home outside Evergreen, Colorado. Pastor had given him up over the weekend as the mastermind behind the plot, and the plan was to arrest him before the markets opened in New York that Monday.

Johnson had loaded almost $10 billion worth of trades into the system and was waiting for the inevitable market plunge that would accompany a weekend of chaos in the U.S. that would leave global investors wondering whether the vaunted American democracy was still standing. Asian and European markets were already reeling.

Shorting stocks. Buying gold and crypto. Leveraged derivatives tied to U.S. interest rates. He was ready to make the killing of his life. Within an hour of the markets opening, he would be among the five or ten richest men in the world.

The FBI had formed a ring around Johnson's home about a half mile away and had gradually been tightening it. As the sun began to come up, they moved in. Ramsey crouched down and moved toward the back deck overlooking the gardens, keeping his eye trained on the

French glass doors that would open into Johnson's cavernous wooden study.

As agents swooped into the house from all sides, Ramsey could see the television screens on news channels, but there was no reaction inside the house. The figure behind the screens kept staring straight at them, as if frozen with greedy anticipation. One agent crashed through a side window as three others barreled through the ornate study door, slamming it into a column of ancient manuscripts as they rolled into the suite

But Johnson didn't move. His eyes stared vacantly at the computer screens, which were now beaming green with his riches from his trades, as the markets plunged at the open in New York. A small trickle of blood ran down the right side of his chin from his mouth. Ramsey could see the agents lower their weapons but didn't know what was going on. He stepped closer, gun still held high at his chest, and then he saw it.

Lying broken on the porch, like a small child's bike discarded hastily in the driveway, an eagle's face staring up at him with one eye. The gun barrel still pointing toward the house. The drone had discharged a single shot before it was deactivated and fell where it hovered. Just the one, cutting a perfect, tiny circle in the glass door before thumping through the leather high-back chair, and into the base of the skull of—by this morning—one of the world's richest men.

Ramsey knelt down and turned it over. The eagle's head fell off the top and rolled toward the house. He slapped the handle and shook out a sleeve of bullets. It had been a killing machine. But unlike the others, this one had completed its last mission. He thought of Johnson sitting there, watching the chaos Friday night and counting the minutes until the markets opened Monday. He never knew what hit him.

"Semper Fi," Ramsey said to himself, and walked into the study, re-holstering his firearm

Conclusion

The sun shone bright that January morning as President-Elect Virginia Robinson placed her left hand on a special Bible, raised her right, and took the oath of the President of the United States on the back porch of the U.S. Capitol before an estimated one million people.

Ramsey and Hoken sat down below the porch, and the marine band, in a VIP section with members of the press and other dignitaries. Behind them a sea of red, white, and blue stretched all the way back to the Washington Monument, and beyond that the Lincoln Memorial.

Hoken gazed up at the flag flying from the top of the Capitol and listened as the band played "My Country, 'Tis of Thee." Somehow, democracy had survived again. Somehow, the violent, bloody, gun-toting experiment that was America, which had lasted more than two hundred fifty years through war, terrorism, and racial hatred, had emerged once again. Shaking off its past and staring proudly and unapologetically into the sun as a new president took her oath.

"And I will work with every breath and beat of my heart to ensure that the gun violence that has plagued this great nation for so long finally, finally comes to an end," Robinson said in her speech.

Hoken turned back to marvel at the sea of smiling, cheering faces. She smiled and gazed into Ramsey's eyes, then up into the skies. Soaring over the celebration of democracy, in perfect formation, it was impossible to ignore the squadron of five hundred armed drones, painted red, white, and blue with American eagle heads at the end of their gun barrels, keeping new watch over a promised but deadly land.

THE END